His to Seduce

Elena Aitken

His to Seduce: Bears of Grizzly Ridge, 2

Ink Blot Communications
ISBN: 978-1-927968-45-1

Also by Elena

Grizzly Ridge
His to Protect
His to Seduce
His to Claim (Spring 2016)

The Springs
Summer of Change
Falling Into Forever
Winter's Burn
Midnight Springs
Second Glances
She's Making A List

Stone Summit Series
Summit of Desire
Summit of Seduction
Summit of Passion

For all my readers who have taken a chance on the Jackson brothers and their stories with me.

CHAPTER ONE

For Chloe Karrington, there was nothing better than walking through the forest: The way the sun danced and played in the branches of the pines as she walked. The cushion of the needles beneath her feet. The fresh, crisp air she inhaled deeply into her lungs.

No. There was nothing better than a walk through the forest.

Unless it was a run.

She glanced around. She was alone.

She could shift into her bear. The need to release her animal bristled just below the surface, but she pushed it down. There were certain things she could do, and certain things she couldn't. And letting her bear loose in an unknown forest was most definitely in the *couldn't* category.

But maybe…

She let her mind drift as she checked out her surroundings.

No one was around. And she already knew there were bears on Grizzly Ridge. Besides the obviousness of the name, it was well known in the bear community that the Jackson brothers had been exiled from their clan and had settled on the ridge instead. Besides, no one would see her if she was careful.

"No." She stamped her foot to make her point. "Pull it together, Chloe. You're working."

She straightened her shoulders, and flipped her dark braid over her shoulder. If there was one thing Chloe prided herself on, it was her professionalism. As an environmental impact researcher, she took her job extremely seriously. Especially considering the very thing she always seemed to find herself researching was the very habitat she craved the most. That, and if she did screw up, the effects could be very serious. Maybe even life-threatening. Chloe flipped open her leather-bound notebook and stared at the newspaper clipping she'd taped into the cover as a constant reminder.

Her fingers traced the faded photo of little Jordan Adams. Only five years old.

Yes, she reminded herself. There were consequences to making mistakes. Mistakes she'd never make again.

She liked to be reminded of the past, but only to the extent that it kept her on her toes. Mostly, Chloe was happy to put the past behind her. *Way* behind her. She tucked the book back into the canvas cross body bag she always wore and continued to walk.

More than just a recreational hike, this was more of a reconnaissance mission as she made her first journey out onto Grizzly Ridge. Later that afternoon, Chloe would drive up the road, park in front of the buildings and formally introduce herself to the Jackson brothers, who ran the adventure tourism lodge on the ridge. But for the moment, she enjoyed the peace and allowed herself to form her own opinion of the operation. It was a technique she liked to use whenever she had the opportunity. Besides, there was a chance that as soon as she made it known that she was there to investigate complaints of environmental disruption, she might not be Grizzly Ridge's most popular guest. And the opportunity to investigate the area on her own would definitely be gone.

She walked for a few more minutes, letting her mind clear. It didn't take long for Chloe's bear to sneak up toward the surface of her consciousness again. *How long had it been since she'd run?*

Weeks? Months?

Too long. *Way* too long.

Ironically, she'd originally taken the job because of the ability to be outdoors. It had seemed like a good way to satisfy the animal inside her. What she hadn't anticipated was that despite the time outdoors, there was less time to let her bear out than she'd thought. But, as it turned out, there were other benefits to the job. Like being alone. Her family would like nothing more than to see her settle down and have her own cubs. Chloe was lucky her parents weren't traditional in their thinking. They were more than happy for her to pick her own mate.

As long as she picked one.

She shook her head.

The last thing she needed was someone tying her down, telling her what to do and keeping her barefoot and pregnant. *No thanks.*

Ever since she was little, Chloe had been fiercely independent. She could handle herself, and that's exactly what she did. She saw the way her older cousins and sisters changed themselves for the males in their life. Becoming giggly and stupid, pretending they couldn't open jars of pickles. *What was that all about?* She could open her own jar of pickles, thank you very much.

No male needed.

Not that her parents understood that. Which was why her career was perfect. She moved around so much from one job to the next that she'd effectively made herself a very undesirable partner. After all, not many strong, alpha males liked a woman with a serious career. At least none she'd found.

It was the perfect explanation for her mom and dad. For the most part, they seemed to understand, even if they couldn't totally wrap their heads around the idea that Chloe was choosing to be alone.

The thing was, as much as she didn't want to admit it, even to herself…Chloe didn't want to be alone. Not really.

She was so wrapped up in her thoughts as she walked, Chloe hardly noticed that the thick pines were thinning. Not until she stepped out onto the ridge. The blue of the sky stretched out before her; the view of the mountain range took her breath away.

"Wow," was all she could manage to say. It was woefully understated, but there was no word to describe the incredible beauty Mother Nature had laid out before her.

Stunned into silencing her mind, Chloe stood frozen on the ridge and took it all in.

After a few moments of admiring the view, she made a split-second decision. It wasn't the most responsible thing to do, but…screw responsible. She needed to experience this amazing place in all the glory it really had to offer. And there was only one way she knew to do that.

She was careful to fold her clothes and tuck her bag next to a tree. Then, naked, Chloe took a step and stretched her arms up overhead. The moments before she shifted into her bear had always been the only time Chloe was comfortable in her curvy human body. Her thick thighs and ample chest were nothing but a hindrance in her daily life, but in those moments, they felt almost sensuous. And then, a second later, Chloe exhaled and started to run. As she moved, her body morphed seamlessly into a strong, beautiful black bear.

Chloe pushed every thought from her mind and let her lean

muscles stretch with the exertion of the run. The cool wind on the ridge whipped through her fur and the feeling of freedom that flowed through every fiber in her body made her feel alive in a way that nothing else had in months.

Soon, she veered from the ridge and into the cover of the trees, where she scratched her back against the trunk of a tall pine before rolling in the fragrant forest floor. She was so caught up in herself, she didn't hear the animal approach until it was too late.

Luke Jackson stared directly into the bluest eyes he'd ever seen on a black bear. Not that he saw many black bears on his ridge. Or any at all.

But the moment she had heard him approach, she'd flipped over from where she was rolling in the pine needles like a cub and stared him down, baring her teeth to him with a snarl. The fact that there was a strange female black bear who was maybe half the size of his own massive grizzly, and that female stood her ground against him, intrigued Luke. A lot.

But not as much as the scent of her. Fresh and crisp like the pine trees they were surrounded by. But something else, too. A white musk filled the air, and his senses.

Which is why it took him a moment to react the way he should have immediately. Finally, his senses caught up with him. With a roar, Luke reared up on his hind legs in a move that was more threatening than predatory. But he knew it would serve his purpose and scare the intruder away, which is exactly what it did. By the time he'd dropped to all fours, the black bear was gone and to his shock, Luke was disappointed.

Very disappointed.

Luke's role at Grizzly Ridge, the eco-adventure lodge he and his two brothers had opened a few months before, was to lead the hikes and outdoor activities. A perfect fit for him because he'd always felt more at home in the woods than anywhere else. It also meant that he could legitimately sneak away to shift into his bear and run free as frequently as he needed too. Especially now that it was autumn, also known as *bump season*. There weren't many guests for the next few weeks, and the few they had at the moment seemed to be more interested in staying close to the main lodge, also known as the Den.

With his free time, he was supposed to be working on a new fly fishing tour they were going to offer to guests, but that afternoon Luke couldn't resist the urge to let his bear run. As soon as he'd shifted and his senses were heightened, he recognized that something was different. There was an unrecognizable scent. Another bear. He knew the woods better than anyone. Every sound, every shadow…every scent.

And the scent of a female was definitely unusual on Grizzly Ridge. A few months earlier, his older brother, Axel, had taken a mate. Luke had recognized right away that Harper was at least part bear, but she'd been totally unaware of it and had never shifted until after she and Axel had mated. Once she'd discovered her bear, there was no keeping her away from it. Axel and Harper spent a lot of late nights running through the woods. But the scent Luke picked up on was definitely different than Harper's slightly sweeter smell.

This female was different. His blood ran hotter with every breath in. She filled his senses.

It hadn't taken long to track her. If she'd been trying to hide, she'd done a bad job of it. Luke approached quietly, stalking her. It was always best to tread lightly until one knew what he was dealing with. But when he saw what he *was* dealing with—a black bear, who, for all intents and purposes, looked as if she was *playing*—he wasn't sure how to handle it.

And she wasn't just any black bear. She had the most magnificent, shiny dark fur that he'd ever seen. It almost appeared blue where the sun hit it. But not as blue as her eyes. Never before had Luke seen a bear with blue eyes; when she finally noticed him and her gaze locked on his, those eyes flashed with electricity. But it wasn't fear. It was almost a challenge.

A challenge he'd accepted. Although moments after he reared up and roared, causing her to run, he'd regretted it. *It was probably for the best.* At least that's what Luke kept telling himself as he turned and lumbered back in the direction he'd come from. Back to the Den.

Nothing good could come from a female bear. Particularly one   clouded his senses so quickly and completely the way that little black bear had.

No. It was definitely better that she'd run off.

CHAPTER TWO

Once Chloe found her clothes, changed and slung her bag over her shoulder, she walked much faster back to where she'd left her rental car. *How could she have been so stupid?* She never should have broken her rule and shifted while she was working.

Never.

But this place. The ridge. It got to her. She couldn't even explain it. Something in the air created a *need* in her.

"Chloe, you're being stupid," she berated herself and picked up her pace. The quicker she could get back to her car, the better. Not that she thought the grizzly would come after her. If he'd wanted to stop her, he would have already.

Her body shivered at the thought. But not out of fear.

It was something else.

Something Chloe wasn't used to feeling. In fact, it was such a foreign sensation that the bear had elicited in her, it took her a moment to figure out what exactly it was. But when she did, she stopped dead in her tracks.

Desire.

That was ridiculous. She shook her head, her braid flipping back and forth. Chloe didn't *do* desire. Or attraction or…or really, anything to do with sex. Sex led to commitment, which led to a relationship, which always led to giving up everything she ever wanted.

No way. It wasn't happening to her. Not ever. She'd decided a long time ago that the best way to avoid losing her life to a male was to keep them out of her life. In all ways. It had been a technique that had worked well for her, too. After all, it was easy to stay celibate if you didn't know what you were missing.

She reached her car, slipped inside and locked the door behind her, as if that would keep out the feelings that slammed through her.

Deep breaths. One. Two. Three. Breathe in. Breathe out.

She silently repeated the mantra until finally her heart rate slowed and she was once again in control of her body and her emotions.

She tilted the rearview mirror down so she could see her reflection.

"Okay," she said to herself. "It's just another job. You're a professional. You've got this."

There was no doubt the grizzly she'd run into was one of the Jackson brothers. The advantage Chloe had was that they didn't know who she was. There was no reason for them to know she'd been the black bear on their ridge. All she had to do was stay professional.

No problem.

She stuck the key in the ignition and put the car in drive. It was time to go to work.

The first thing Chloe noticed when she pulled up to the main lodge of Grizzly Ridge was how inviting and cozy it looked. Not that it was a small house. Not at all. It was a massive log building with an oversized porch stretched along the front. Huge windows covered the front half of the lodge and a stone chimney stuck out the top of the peaked roof. A wooden sign with *The Den* carved into it was nailed to the porch rail.

"How cute." Chloe shook her head but couldn't help and smile at the Jackson brothers' sense of humor. She allowed herself a moment to look around and take in the rest of the area. Some smaller cabins were set behind the main lodge and over to the left, the start of something was under construction. She made a note to investigate that a little closer. Part of the job was making sure the environment, particularly the native animals, weren't disrupted by any new buildings in the area.

Chloe could have happily sat in the safety of the rental car for a few more minutes, but when the main door of the Den opened and a couple stepped out onto the porch, she knew she was out of time.

She gathered up her bag, shoving a few extra pens inside, and opened the door. "Here goes nothing." She pasted a smile on her face and headed up the steps but she needn't have rushed. The couple out on the porch hadn't even spotted her yet. In fact, judging by their embrace and the way their lips were locked onto each other's, they hadn't noticed much of anything.

Chloe cleared her throat to make her presence known. She had a very low tolerance for any public displays of affection and the last thing she needed was to witness anyone else's passion.

The couple stopped kissing, but didn't release their embrace. Instead, their grip relaxed and they turned, arms still around each other, to greet her.

"Hello." The man smiled. He was tall, dark, and incredibly handsome. "Welcome to Grizzly Ridge. How can I help you today?"

Chloe nodded. "Hi. My name is Chloe Karrington. I'm an investigator for Environmental Energies, a private company that investigates reports of any causes for environmental concern."

The man unwound himself from his partner and crossed his arms over his chest. He still smiled, but Chloe could see the flicker of concern in his eye. It was a look she was familiar with. "Environmental concern?" he asked. "Do you have a reason to be environmentally concerned with Grizzly Ridge?"

"It's not that there *is* a concern," she said. "And that's what I'm here to assess." She smiled as sweetly as possible. From her experience, it was much easier to do her job if she had the cooperation of the subjects under investigation. "I assure you, it's a very preliminary investigation at this point."

"And if we refuse?"

"Axel." The woman put her hand on his arm. "I don't think there's any need to be rude or defensive," she said. "Especially since we know everything on the Ridge has been done with the environment and the animals in mind." She turned and smiled at Chloe. "Hi. I'm Harper and this is Axel Jackson. Please excuse his abruptness. It's been a busy week."

Chloe instantly warmed to the woman and her welcoming manner. She exuded friendship and kindness, and despite the fact that Chloe couldn't remember the last time she'd had a female friend, she wanted to know Harper. She took the woman's outstretched hand and shook it.

"It's nice to meet you." Chloe faced Axel. "I promise, I'm not here to look for trouble. Just to look."

He smiled, albeit a bit more reluctantly, and shook her

hand as well. "I believe you," he said. "You're just doing your job."

"Exactly. Is there somewhere we can talk for a few minutes to get an idea of how I can check things out?"

Axel led them through the doors into the Den. If Chloe thought the outside was spectacular, the inside was even more so. The giant stone fireplace was the centerpiece of the room, with cozy couches scattered around in front of it. She could imagine curling up there with a glass of wine and a good book. The thought came so suddenly out of nowhere it shocked her. A large staircase, presumably to the guest rooms, curled down into the main sitting area. Bookshelves lined some of the walls, as well as tables designed for cards, puzzles, and games. Behind the fireplace, Chloe could see a large family-style dining room and a door she assumed led to the kitchen.

"It's beautiful." It took her a moment to realize she'd spoken aloud, but when Harper smiled and grabbed her arm to give it a squeeze, she blushed at her slip.

"It really is," Harper said. "Why don't you guys start chatting and I'll go grab some snacks from Kade?"

Chloe waited until Harper disappeared into the kitchen and turned to Axel. "She's lovely. Your wife—"

"Mate."

He might as well have smacked her for the shock that radiated through her at the word. She cleared her throat. "Pardon?"

If Axel had meant to shock her, it worked, but there was no sign of maliciousness on his face. He was grinning and obviously trying not to laugh. "I can't figure out what clan you're from," he said. "But I sensed it on you right away. I assumed you'd figured us out as well."

Chloe nodded. "The Jackson brothers are kind of well-known in the community." She shrugged an apology, but

Axel nodded his agreement. It was no secret they'd been banished by their grandfather and cast out of their clan. It was good to see they weren't sensitive about it. At least Axel wasn't. "But I didn't realize Harper was—"

"She's half-blooded. It's not easy to spot."

That made sense. Once they got the formalities out of the way, Chloe launched into the reason for her visit and what she would need from the Jackson brothers, which was mostly access to the land and buildings. Axel turned out to be very receptive and easy to talk to. By the time Harper came back with a tray of cookies, with a man behind her with a carafe of coffee, they'd already made the preliminary arrangements.

"Chloe, I'd like you to meet my youngest brother, Kade." She stood and shook the man's hand. He was large like his brother, but even though he was slightly shorter, he was far more intimidating than Axel. A tattoo of something tribal snaked down one arm, and despite his smile, there was an edge to him. "She's here to make sure we're doing everything right by the environment up here. I assume you'll be staying with us, Chloe."

"Oh, I…I actually booked into a ranch down the road."

"The ranch?" Kade scoffed. "I don't think so."

"I assumed you were booked already." That was only partly true. Of course, there was a chance that the Ridge might be booked, but mostly she wasn't sure it would be a great idea for her to stay at the location she was investigating. However, now that she was here and saw how inviting the Den was, not to mention the people, she definitely had second thoughts.

"You can't stay at Blackwood Ranch," Kade was saying. "It's run by a bunch of damn wolves. You'll stay right here. We have extra room, don't we, Axel?"

Axel nodded. "Not that there's anything wrong with the

wolves." He gave his brother a look. "But Kade's right. You should stay here. It's bump season. There aren't a lot of guests right now—we have lots of room."

"I don't know…I probably shouldn't—"

"Nonsense," Harper said. "I can't see any reason why you shouldn't stay with us. Besides, it would be nice to have another woman around."

"You have plenty of women around with our guests," Axel said.

"This is different." Before Chloe could protest again, Harper jumped up from the couch where she'd been sitting with her mate and grabbed Chloe's hand. "I insist that you stay with us. Come on, I'll show you your room."

Luke finished putting away the last of the mountain bikes in the shed and wiped his hands on the legs of his jeans. It had been an unexpectedly busy afternoon. He'd misjudged their current guests. They seemed like the types who would prefer to stay close to the Den, enjoying the cool fall days from the comfort of the porch. That certainly wasn't the case when they found out Luke had just added a small fleet of mountain bikes as part of the adventure center. He'd also added the name—adventure center—to the small shed where he kept the outdoor equipment. It was an idea Axel had initially scoffed at, but Luke had been right. When the guests thought there was an added sense of adventure to their activities, they were definitely more likely to sign up for them.

That had definitely been the case with the Wesleys and Coopers, the two couples he'd just had out biking on the trails. It had been a fun afternoon, and everyone was exhausted when they'd returned. Including Luke. All he wanted to do was grab his dinner to go and spend the night alone in his cabin.

Maybe then he'd allow himself a moment to think about that little black bear he'd stumbled across earlier.

No.

He'd managed to keep her out of his head all day; he wasn't about to let her into his thoughts now. Not until he was alone.

But first—food.

His t-shirt was soaked through with perspiration and clung to his chest, so he stripped it off and tossed it in the corner of the shed, before exchanging it with a clean flannel button-up. Luke glanced down at his muddy jeans. He didn't have any spares in the adventure center; they would have to do. Harper would definitely have something to say about his appearance, that was for sure.

He laughed and shook his head at the way his brother's mate had so quickly taken on a role of mother bear with all of them. Not that it mattered much; in fact, he wouldn't admit it but Luke kind of liked it. It was nice to have a female care, even if it was different than the way she cared for his brother.

Not for the first time, Luke's thoughts drifted to the idea of a mate. Maybe Axel *was* onto something? Maybe a mate wasn't such a bad thing after all?

As quickly as the idea popped into his head, he dismissed it. Of course having a mate was a bad idea. Look at what happened with his parents. His mother had been cast out of the clan for finding a mate who wasn't from an *approved* clan. At least that was the story their grandfather told them. Not that Luke could ask for more details, even if he wanted to. The Jackson brothers had also been cast out of their clan. Their offense? Failing to bring back their sister, Kade's twin, after she'd fallen in love and run away with her own mate.

No. Mating was a bad idea.

No matter how much Luke's bear might be telling him different.

He flicked off the light and closed up the adventure center before he headed straight to the Den and the delicious aroma of Kade's pot roast.

Everyone was already sitting around the large wooden table when Luke walked through the doors. Guests of Grizzly Ridge all ate together family style, and more often than not the Jackson brothers all joined them.

"Sorry I'm late." Luke walked closer. The food smelled amazing, and a little different than Kade's usual pot roast. "It smells fantastic, Kade. Did you do something different today? There's something almost—"

He couldn't finish his thought. All Luke's attention was focused on the woman next to Harper. She was shorter, and her back had been facing him, so he hadn't seen her at first, but when she turned in her chair, Luke couldn't see anyone but her.

She was gorgeous. Short, but deliciously plump. Her breasts were heavy and filled out the button-up denim shirt she wore. The top button was undone, giving Luke an enticing view of what hid beneath the fabric. And judging by the swell of cleavage that was making his mouth water, that was a whole lot.

But it wasn't just her breasts that attracted his gaze. Her hair. So black it was almost blue. Just like the—*no. It couldn't be.*

The black bear he'd seen in the woods.

Luke's eyes locked on hers. Her very blue, very electric eyes. The bluest eyes he'd ever seen. Except for the ones he'd seen in the forest earlier.

"You're the—"

"Chloe Karrington." She rose and extended her hand. The smile on her face was sweet, but there was a warning in her eyes Luke didn't miss. "I'm the environmental..."

Luke didn't catch the rest of what she said, or if she said anything at all, because the only thing he could focus on was the searing heat that shot through his hand and straight to his groin when he took her hand. He squeezed her hand tighter, and without really realizing what he was doing, pulled her closer to him until they were only inches apart. Her scent filled his nostrils, choking off his ability to extract any oxygen from the air around him. But he didn't need it. All he needed was this female in front of him. Needed her in a way that caused every cell in his body to vibrate on a frequency he'd never experienced.

It took him a moment to realize Axel was speaking and had somehow worked his way between Luke and the female he very badly needed to claim.

"Chloe is here to investigate some claims about the environmental impact of Grizzly Ridge." Axel angled himself so he was firmly between Luke and Chloe. Reluctantly, Luke released her hand and immediately felt its absence. He tried to look around his big brother but he couldn't see her face before she sat down. He did notice that she clasped her hands tightly in her lap and the action sent a thrill through him.

What the hell was wrong with him? He never reacted to females. *Never.* Not beyond a quick and dirty hookup with a local in town. But that was just enough to scratch an itch and keep his bear satisfied. It had nothing to do with the way he felt at the moment. Nothing.

"Luke?"

He shook his head and looked to his brother, who stared at him, obviously waiting for an answer to an unheard question.

"What?" He realized a second too late he'd snapped at Axel.

If his brother noticed, he didn't say anything. "I just asked if you'd be okay showing Chloe around the ridge for the purposes of her research."

"No."

The answer was out of his mouth before he even realized what he'd said. It shocked no one quite as much as it did him, but it was the right answer. The *only* answer. Nothing good could come from a female who affected him as much as this one had in such a short time. There was no way in hell he was going to be alone with her.

"Busy," he grunted, and without even acknowledging their paying guests, he turned and stormed into the kitchen. He would have left straight away, but his bear was growling with hunger. If he had any chance of controlling himself, which was becoming less and less likely, he'd need to eat something.

Luke grabbed a dish and piled roast on it. Behind him, he heard the door swing open. "I'm not in the mood," he growled.

"Is that a generalization? Or is it specifically directed to me?"

Chloe could see the way his back tensed at the sound of her voice, and something akin to a thrill ran through her. She knew the moment he'd walked into the Den that he was the bear she'd seen in the woods. Her body had reacted instantly to his presence.

Damn.

And it was clear to anyone with eyes in their head that he'd reacted to her, too. *Hard.*

It was dangerous.

Which was why the last thing she should do was leave the relative safety of the dining room table in order to seek him out. Despite knowing that she should stay put and do her best to ignore the way he'd looked at her, the way his touch felt on her bare skin, the way her entire body had come alive just by standing near him, she couldn't.

Chloe braced herself against the wall, needing the solid reassurance to keep herself together. She waited for him to answer her and she didn't have to wait long. Luke turned. His movement was slow and deliberate. When his eyes locked on hers, Chloe was glad to be leaning against the wall because she was pretty sure her legs wouldn't have supported her under the scrutiny of his gaze.

"It's a generalization." His voice was rough, strained.

Chloe swallowed hard, forcing herself to remain unaffected by the deliciously gorgeous man in front of her despite the fact that she could see the need flaring in his eyes. She'd practiced her cool, uncaring demeanor for just such a scenario. Well, not really, but it certainly would come in handy. At least it *would* if she could keep it together. It didn't look promising.

"But I think it could be applied…" Luke left the counter and slowly made his way across the large kitchen toward her. With every step he took, Chloe's heart beat a little faster. When he was close enough that she could feel his heat, her breath was coming in short puffs. Her skin was flushed and it suddenly was way too hot in the kitchen. She glanced behind her. The door was within reach. All she had to do was turn and leave.

But that's not why she'd followed him.

"Specifically to you." Luke came to a stop only inches from Chloe. She worked to control her breathing. No way would she let this man see how he affected her. More specifically—no way would she let her body *be* affected.

She straightened her shoulders and pushed down any and all desire she felt. "Me?" She tried to keep her voice light. She failed. "Why would I have anything to do with your mood?" Chloe tipped her head and raised her eyebrows in a way she hoped was more bitchy than flirty. But judging by the way desire flared in Luke's eyes and consequently through her body at his reaction, she failed.

"You know damn well why."

Before Chloe could react, Luke's hands were on her: one on her cheek, cupping her face with its massive width; the other twined in her hair as he pulled her roughly toward him. It was a possessive move. A move that screamed of ownership. Her emotions jangled into a big, mixed-up mess. She should be offended, outraged at his nerve. But the moment his lips pressed to hers, all Chloe could feel was a deep, instinctual need for this man who kissed her with an urgency she'd never before experienced.

Her own arms wrapped around his strong back; her fingers dug into his muscle in an effort to bring him closer to her. A moan escaped her lips; Luke growled in response and pressed himself against her so she could feel his hard need for her.

The feel of him against her soft belly sparked something in Chloe and a surge of panic washed through her. She pulled her hands away and pressed them against his hard chest before shoving him hard.

"No." She shook her head and touched her fingers to her lips, more in an effort to remember the taste and feel of him than to wipe it away. "I...we can't do this."

"Yes we can." Luke took a step toward her again, but she backed away and looked down. She couldn't look at the heat in his eyes. If she did, there was no doubt she'd be lost in him again and there was no way that could happen.

"No," she said as firmly as she could manage. "We can't." She took three quick steps until there was enough distance between them before she added, "In fact, I think it would be a good idea if you left me alone to do my job." She knew she sounded cold, but it was what she needed. Chloe looked away before he could see the lie in her eyes when she said, "After all, that's the only reason I'm here. Nothing more."

CHAPTER THREE

Chloe managed to avoid Luke for the next two days, mostly. They'd bumped into each other a few times in the Den on the occasions where she couldn't manage a viable excuse as to why she didn't want to eat in the dining room with everyone else. Besides that, it was a lie. She enjoyed the company of Axel and Harper. Even Kade, the youngest of the Jackson brothers, was friendly, if not a bit growly. And not only was he an amazing chef, he was also incredibly passionate about it. Something else was going on with Kade; it was clear to anyone who paid attention, particularly another bear with heightened senses.

Not that Chloe's senses were heightened. At least that's what she kept telling herself. It was easier to lie to herself than to admit that she'd been a mess of feelings, hormones, and something else she wasn't quite sure how to pin down, ever since she'd met Luke. Never mind the kiss they'd shared.

Oh, the kiss. Despite her bravado and trying to pretend it didn't matter, it did. A lot.

Which was exactly why she needed to stay away from him. She'd lived her entire life avoiding a mate or even the pretense of a mate. The last thing Chloe needed was to be tied down to a male. She was an independent woman with a life of her own. She had goals and dreams; she didn't need anything screwing that up.

Or enhancing it.

That annoying little voice in her head kept trying to chime in with reasons she should stop avoiding Luke and give in to their connection. But that little voice didn't know anything. Not really.

If the others noticed anything awkward between her and Luke, they didn't mention it to Chloe. To her surprise, they let her conduct her investigation in relative peace, without looking over her shoulder or tracking her every move the way other subjects of her investigations usually did. Of course, those people usually had something to hide. The more Chloe dug into operations at Grizzly Ridge, the more she was convinced the Jacksons didn't have anything to hide. Of course, her investigation had focused primarily around documentation and building plans, as well as the independent environmental consults the Jacksons had done before beginning construction. From what she could tell, they'd not only followed protocol, but went above and beyond to protect the environment of the ridge. Not that she would expect anything less from bears, but she couldn't exactly put that in her report.

No, she'd have to be thorough. And that would include touring the grounds thoroughly before she signed off on any recommendation. She'd more or less exhausted what she could do indoors. More than exhausted, really. She was dragging her feet because going out to check out the property would mean being with Luke. Alone. She'd used the last few days to pull herself together and get control of her raging feelings. Not that it was working. It most definitely wasn't.

There was a knock at the door of the office she was

working in. Chloe quickly sat up straight in an effort to look as if she wasn't in fact daydreaming about the taste of Luke's lips on her own. "Come in."

The door cracked open and Harper stuck her head around the corner. "I thought you could use a break," she said. "Can I steal you away for a bit?"

Chloe closed her notebook and stretched her arms overhead. "Absolutely. I was just thinking that I could use a little break. What did you have in mind?"

"Shopping."

"Shopping?" There was definitely nowhere to shop at Grizzly Ridge. As far as Chloe could tell, they didn't even have a gift shop, and the little town she'd passed on her way through didn't look as though it had much in the way of shops to choose from.

"Well, calling it shopping is a bit of a stretch, but there are a few shops and I'm dying to have some girl time." Chloe could only laugh at Harper's enthusiasm. As a general rule, she liked being alone, but she supposed she could understand how Harper might get lonely.

"Of course," she said, finding herself actually happy for the distraction. She wasn't a big shopper, or really a big fan of girl time at all, but she liked Harper and an afternoon off could be fun.

That was it. Luke couldn't take one more day of having Chloe so close and all at the same time, so damn far away. He'd spent the morning walking the stream, casting his line and only halfheartedly attempting to catch any of the trout that were there in abundance. If he'd wanted to, there was no doubt he would have been able to rack up a nice lot of fresh fish for Kade to cook up for dinner. But he couldn't focus on which fly to tie on, or even pay attention to where he was casting his line. For an accomplished fisherman, it was embarrassing.

Which was why he needed to get her out of his system. And it couldn't wait.

As soon as he'd stashed his rod, fishing vest, and tackle box in the shed, Luke had stormed down to the Den, ready to confront Chloe and the growing tension between them. It didn't matter that they hadn't really spoken since their kiss. They hadn't needed to. The heat from that kiss had sustained him for the last few days simply because once his lips touched hers, he'd known. *She was his.* It was only a matter of time.

The moment he walked into the Den, he knew she wasn't there. Her scent lingered on the air, just the way her presence did in his mind, but it didn't fill his senses the way it did when she was near. He tried not to be disappointed, but his entire body felt the absence of her like a physical ache. He headed in the direction of the kitchen; he might as well eat while he was there. Besides, it had been awhile since he'd checked in with his brothers. And no doubt they'd have something to say about that.

"I need something to eat," he greeted his youngest brother Kade, who stood over the stove, stirring something that smelled fantastic.

"Hi to you, too." Kade didn't bother turning around. "It's not ready yet. You'll have to wait."

A growl rose up, but Luke swallowed it back. If he didn't get at least one of the things he wanted, and soon, he was going to have a hard time controlling his bear. And considering Chloe was neither nearby nor overly pleased by his attentions, food seemed like his best bet for the moment.

"Settle down," Kade said. "Here." He tossed him a

fresh roll that Luke caught easily. "The stew will be done in a few minutes, but it's for lunch tomorrow."

"You won't miss a bowl." Luke bit into the bun and sat on one of the high stools at the counter. The kitchen was set up to be state-of-the-art while keeping the comfortable, inviting atmosphere the rest of the Den had. The idea was, if guests wanted to pop into the kitchen for a cup of coffee or a snack, they should feel welcome at all times. And despite how growly Kade had become over the last few months, it seemed to be an idea that worked. At least Kade was reserving his bad attitude mostly to his brothers and putting on a pretty good face for the guests. Mostly.

What Kade really needed was to go spend some time with his bear, but Luke didn't even bother to bring it up. It wasn't a secret that Kade had denied his bear ever since their little sister, Kira, Kade's twin, had run off with her mate. Kade didn't believe in mates. Let alone fated mates. As far as he was concerned, the very idea of such a thing had ruined their family. Luke couldn't figure out why his little brother thought it would change anything by denying the animal inside him, but he clearly wanted to punish himself for something that was definitely not his fault.

"Give it fifteen minutes," Kade said grudgingly. "Then you can have a bowl. But that's it. The last thing I need is to make another batch because you couldn't control yourself."

Luke bristled. "I can control myself just fine." He straightened on his stool.

Kade came around the counter and pushed his shirt sleeves up past his elbows.

Luke raised an eyebrow. "Another new one?" He gestured to the tattoos that covered his brother's arms.

"Awhile ago," Kade grunted. "Not that any of you would have noticed."

"Really?" Luke had to try hard not to laugh at his brother's petulance. "Are you not getting the attention you need, little brother?"

Kade growled and tightened his hand into a fist. *Good.* He welcomed the fight. He needed a release from the torture that was Chloe. Beating the shit out of his brother wasn't ideal, but it was something. And he'd take what he could get.

"Don't think that because you're sniffing around some female that you're better than me, brother." Kade drew out the last word just to taunt Luke. It worked. He jumped up from the stool so fast that it clattered to the tile floor behind him.

"What did you say?"

"You heard me." Kade sneered. "And clearly this is what you're looking for. Hit me. If you can't close the deal with her, you might as well—"

Luke didn't hear the rest of what Kade said. A roaring, like a white static noise, filled his ears and his vision completely clouded with fury. Brother or not, there was no way he was going to sit by while Kade spoke like that. *Not about his mate.* He pulled his arm back, ready to connect his fist with Kade's smug face, but when he threw the punch, something stopped him.

Luke's vision cleared instantly and locked on Axel's unimpressed face. His hand was locked around Luke's forearm like a vise. "Does someone want to tell me what happened?" he asked. "Because I have to think there's a really damn good reason you'd both be fighting like boys in the schoolyard in the middle of the kitchen. When we have guests." Axel glared at them both in turn, his hard eyes finally landing on Luke. A second later, his mouth curled up in a smirk. "I don't think I even need to ask what this is all about."

The drive down the mountain was windy and tricky in places, but Harper handled the truck like a pro and they made it into town in little under an hour. "This is it," Harper said as they drove down the main street. "Boulder Creek isn't much, but it's usually all we need here. And if we really need something more, Jacksonville is only another thirty minutes east."

"Jacksonville? As in…"

Harper nodded. "As in the Jackson brothers? You got it. It's a long story, though, so don't ask. All that matters is that we do most of our shopping right here in Boulder Creek."

There was clearly a story there, but Chloe knew enough not to ask. After all, it didn't matter. Not really. Harper and she weren't friends, not really, and she was only there on assignment. As soon as she was done with her research, she was leaving. Even if the idea of that felt a little less appealing all the time. Especially considering it meant no Luke.

That was a ludicrous idea. She couldn't even think about it. Besides, it wasn't as if they'd even spent any time together. Quite the opposite, really. She'd done everything in her power to avoid Luke because her entire body lit up whenever he was in the room. All she wanted to do was to be in his arms again and have those lips on hers just one more time. But once more wouldn't be enough. Not nearly enough. Her bear wanted more.

"Chloe?" She blinked hard and focused on Harper, who stared at her, obviously waiting for an answer.

"Sorry." She smiled apologetically. "I was daydreaming about something."

"I noticed." Harper grinned knowingly. "I thought we could pop in here really quick," she said. "If you're not too busy daydreaming, that is."

Chloe blushed. By the look on the other woman's face, Harper knew exactly what—or in this case, who—she was daydreaming about.

"I'm good. Let's go shopping." She pushed past Harper into the little boutique store and immediately busied herself digging through the racks before Harper could question her further.

The store was small, but it turned out to be full of super cute things. The racks were stuffed with unique tops, skirts, and sweaters. Despite the fact that Chloe usually avoided shopping altogether, she found herself grabbing item after item until she was loaded down with a pile of things to try on.

"This store is unreal," she said to Harper, who was collecting her own large pile of clothes.

"It's great, right? Bree designs them all herself and since she's a curvy girl like us..."

Chloe's eyes drifted over to Bree, who besides greeting them when they walked in, had left them largely on their own to shop in peace. She was at a desk in the corner, madly sketching in a notepad. At the mention of her name, she put her pencil down and joined them.

"These are all so beautiful." Chloe held up her arm and the stack of clothes she'd gathered.

"Thank you." Bree blushed and took the clothes from Chloe. "I'll put them in a room for you to try on. I hope you find something that fits."

"I'm sure I will," Chloe said. "They all look like they're going to fit perfectly. I think my problem will be choosing which ones to buy. It's so rare to find such nice things in my size."

"Right?" Harper nodded her agreement. "Bree's store has been a total blessing."

"I don't understand, though." Chloe looked around the little store, whose name, the Bree Hive, made a lot more sense now that she'd met Bree. "I don't mean this to sound rude," she continued, "but how can you have a business like this in such a small town? I mean, it doesn't seem like there are really enough people in Boulder Creek to support it."

Bree laughed. "There's not. But it also makes retail space super cheap. And to be honest, the retail portion of my business is really quite minor. I sell mostly online."

"Online? That's fantastic." Chloe had moved into the change room that was made up of thick curtains breaking off some private areas. She was already accumulating a pile of items she *had* to have. "So I can order when I get home, too? I hate shopping, but your clothes fit me perfectly." She turned and admired her reflection in the mirror. The royal-blue tunic she had on slid over her curves in a way that enhanced all the right places while at the same time minimizing the ones she wanted minimized.

"What do you mean when you go home?" Harper was in the next curtain, but a moment later, her face popped around the thick fabric. "You're not really going to go home, are you?"

Chloe bit her tongue against a comment regarding boundaries, because something told her it would be ignored anyway. "I don't understand," she said. "Of course I'm going home. Why wouldn't I?"

Even as she answered Harper, she knew what the other woman was going to say, and she didn't want to hear it.

"Chloe." Harper walked right into Chloe's changing area. "You can't leave," she said slowly. "You're Luke's mate."

All the air was sucked from her lungs, and her legs buckled beneath her. Yes, she knew on some level there was an attraction between them. On some, very obvious level. *But mate? No.* Chloe didn't *do* mates. Not even when every cell in her body yearned to be with Luke. To be in his arms. In his bed. In his—

"I don't mate."

"You don't mate?"

"No."

"You mean you haven't mated."

"No," Chloe said slowly. "I mean, I don't mate. I won't."

"Because you hadn't found him until now."

"No."

Chloe needed the conversation to be over. She gathered up a stack of clothes, including the ones she'd worn into the store, and hauled them out of the changing room and to the front desk. Harper was right behind her.

"You do know that Luke is your—"

"Client." She said the word firmly and pointed with her eyes to Bree, who rang up her purchases and tried not to laugh. From what Chloe understood, Harper was only half bear and still fairly new to the whole idea of it. *But surely she must know the rules.* They couldn't talk about mates or shifting or anything else in front of humans. It wasn't done.

"Oh, Bree knows." Harper waved her unspoken concerns away. "After all, she grew up here."

Bree nodded. "It's true."

"I'm still not talking about it." Chloe crossed her arms over her chest. "Besides, there's nothing to talk about."

"Like hell." Harper touched her arm and something inside Chloe snapped.

"No!" She jerked away and grabbed up her bag of purchases that Bree handed her. "There's nothing to talk about, Harper, because there's nothing going on between me and Luke. Whatever you *think* about mating, or me, you're wrong. You don't know me. So back off."

Without waiting for a response, Chloe stormed out of the store and let the glass door with the tinkly bells slam shut behind her.

Luke shook his brother's hand off him and turned away to pull himself together. He'd done a good job hiding his feelings for Chloe from everyone. Or at least he thought he had. The last thing he needed was his brother's opinions interfering in the middle of whatever the hell was going on with him.

"Don't bother trying to deny it." Luke could hear the laughter in Axel's voice behind him. It sparked a fury deep in his gut. "I've been there, remember. There's nothing you can do about it."

"That's bullshit." He shook his head. He'd spent the last few days trying to figure out a way to have Chloe while at the very same time trying to figure out how to get her out of his head. More than that, he needed to figure out how to get her out of his entire system.

"It's not bullshit," Axel said, no longer trying to hide his laughter. "It's fate."

"Fuck off."

Luke turned, and both he and Axel stared at Kade, who looked as though he was barely containing his anger. If Luke didn't know better, he would think Kade was about to let his bear loose right there in the kitchen. The fact that he wasn't was both impressive and more than a little frightening. Kade shook his head hard. "You think you found your mate, too?" He spat the question at Luke.

He couldn't answer the question. There was no doubt that Chloe was his mate, but it was more complicated than simply feeling something. Besides, he knew exactly what Kade was thinking. It wasn't long ago, when Axel found his mate in Harper, that Luke felt very similar things. "It doesn't change anything here," Luke said.

"To hell it doesn't." Kade spun on his heel and slammed his way through the kitchen and out the back door, picking up a coffee mug and throwing it at the wall on his way.

Luke waited a beat after he left before he exhaled.

"He'll get over it." Axel moved silently through the kitchen, the laughter gone, and cleaned up the broken pieces of mug. "He's still sensitive about...well..."

"Mates?"

Axel nodded.

Not only did Kade blame the idea of fated mates on losing his twin sister, but also for the loss of their parents. The twins had been too young to remember their parents when the brothers were returned to their grandfather and the Jackson clan. They'd given up their father's name, as well as their parents. Their grandfather never spoke of it and now that they'd been cast out of their clan as well, there as a good chance they'd never know. Not that it mattered much to the older brothers. Only Kade seemed to hold onto the past that couldn't be changed. He blamed all of his life's problems on mates. Ironically, it was Kade who'd benefit the most from finding a female of his own, to calm his bear that was clearly on the verge of getting out of control.

"We need to do something about him," Luke said. "He's getting worse."

Axel nodded and shrugged in the same move. "He's grown. We can't force him to let go of the past. We can't force him to do anything. Besides, we're not talking about Kade right now."

"Yes we are." Luke stalked over to the now unattended stove. *Screw it.* He was hungry. He took the lid off the pot of stew and grabbed a ladle.

"It's pretty crazy, isn't it?"

Luke didn't pretend not to know what Axel was talking about. "I'm not talking about it."

"But it is, right?"

Luke finished doling out his stew and returned to the counter. Instead of answering his brother, he shoved a spoonful in his mouth.

"Look, Luke. I'm not trying to be an asshole, but—"

"Then don't be."

He didn't turn, but he could hear Axel sigh next to him. "A mate is a good thing, Luke."

"She's not my mate." He dropped his spoon into the bowl with a clatter. "She won't even talk to me. She's been avoiding me for days. So even if she is my *mate*, I wouldn't even know." *Except he did.* "Isn't it supposed to go both ways?"

Axel reclined against the wall and crossed his arms. "There aren't any rules."

Luke glared at him.

"There aren't," Axel said again. "And if there are, I don't know them."

"Then what is there?"

Axel laughed.

"What?"

"It's instinct."

Instinct?

The stew tasted like cardboard in his mouth. He couldn't eat. He couldn't sit. He couldn't think. He pushed away from the counter and like his little brother had before him, Luke stormed out of the kitchen. Only, unlike his little brother, Luke was going to do something about the animal inside him that was practically ripping and clawing to be let out. If he didn't do something about it soon, his bear would destroy him.

CHAPTER FOUR

She'd been a total bitch and she knew it. Harper had only been trying to be friendly. Chloe knew that. After they left Bree's Knees, Harper had run into the drugstore to make a purchase and they'd headed back up the mountain. She'd wanted to stop in at the coffee shop and buy Harper a latte so she could apologize for her behavior, but something stopped her. Her pride, mostly.

And the fact that even though it pissed her off to admit it, Chloe was afraid Harper might be right about Luke. It wasn't the first time she'd considered it. Not by a long shot. But she'd done a good job ignoring her feelings so far, and she couldn't let a woman she barely knew send her off the rails now.

No. She'd stick to her resolve. She didn't want a mate. She wouldn't take a mate. *Not now. Not ever.*

Probably.

It was that probably that kept Chloe from asking Harper to stop for a coffee. It kept her from apologizing to the other woman, and it even kept her from making polite conversation, which led to a very quiet, very strained drive to Grizzly Ridge. Something else Chloe felt guilty about.

When they pulled up to the main building, Harper turned the key in the ignition and let out a deep breath. "Look, Chloe. I just—"

"You don't need to apologize."

"Apologize?"

"Yes. For being so rude in the store." Even as the words came out of her mouth, Chloe knew she was being a class-A asshole. Harper had nothing to apologize for, and they both knew it.

Harper opened her mouth and shut it again before she pressed her lips into a thin line. Chloe could feel her heart break a little. This woman was the closest thing she'd had to a friend since she'd been a child. And she'd liked it. A lot. Which was why it hurt so bad when instead of saying anything else to her, Harper sighed and got out of the truck, leaving Chloe sitting alone.

She waited a few moments until Harper disappeared up the path toward the cabin she shared with Axel behind the main lodge. When the other woman was finally out of view, Chloe gathered up her bags and went inside. She was starving, and the smell of something delicious coming from the kitchen was almost enough to entice her to stay downstairs. Dinner would be served in a little over an hour, but there was no way she could sit at the table across from Harper after the way she'd treated her. She needed to apologize, Chloe knew that, but something stopped her. *What was the point really?* After all, she was just there to do a job. Then she'd leave, and the Jackson brothers and Harper and all her crazy talk about mates would be out of her life.

Or would it?

Harper's words repeated in her head like a broken record, just the way they had the moment she'd spoken them. And it pissed her off because despite the fact that she didn't want to believe there was any truth in what the other woman had said, Chloe knew there was.

Before she could sneak upstairs, the door to the kitchen swung open, startling her. She turned, half expecting to see Luke there. It was Kade. Disappointment washed through her.

"Hungry?" he asked her.

Chloe nodded. "I am, but I'm afraid I can't join you for dinner. Is there any way I can grab a sandwich to take upstairs?"

"A sandwich?" He wrinkled his brow and his eyes narrowed as if she'd personally offended him, which she likely had. "There's no way you're eating a sandwich when I just spent all afternoon roasting chickens. I'll fix you a plate and have it brought up later."

"Thank you." He really was a sweet guy under that rough exterior. She took a step up the stairs before she turned around again. "Could you please tell Axel that I've done all I can do in here? I'll need to get outside and investigate the grounds tomorrow."

Kade grunted. "I'll tell Luke," he said, with something like hesitation in his voice.

"No. You don't have to tell Luke."

"I do," he said simply. "He's the one who'll have to take you around."

"Oh, no, I don't—"

"There's no other choice."

It didn't take much to see that if there had been any other choice, Kade would have taken it, too. He clearly was just as thrilled about the idea of Luke and Chloe spending time together as she was. Which begged a completely different question. Why did it bother *him* so much?

Instinct? Ha.

The word had haunted Luke all afternoon. He'd gone for a run on the ridge, but even that hadn't done much to quell the growing storm inside him. There was only one thing to do.

He needed Chloe. He needed to get her out of his system. It was the only way. If instinct truly was at play the way Axel said it was, surely he'd be able to satisfy whatever was going on if he could only get her in his bed. Just once.

It was a flawed strategy; he knew it. But he was out of options, which was why he found himself holding a tray with a plate of dinner Kade had prepared for her. He'd snuck it away before anyone could protest. That was one delivery he planned to make in person.

He rapped on the door, a sharp sound that filled the empty hallway. He waited for a moment, expecting her to open the door at once. But there was nothing. She hadn't gone downstairs; he would have seen her. Plus, Kade said she was starving. Surely she should be waiting for her dinner?

Luke knocked again. This time he listened closely, but still there was no noise from inside. Except…there it was. A faint, but distinct sound of the bathtub running.

Instantly, the thought of Chloe's naked, wet body covered in foamy bubbles filled his head. The thought was too much. Luke swallowed hard, trying his best to push the image from his brain. He stood for a beat, trying to figure out what he should do. It only took a second to make his decision. If the door was unlocked, he'd simply put the tray down so it was waiting for her.

It was a flawed plan in so many ways, but at that moment it didn't matter.

He tried the doorknob.

It turned.

He grinned at his luck, but at the same time a fierce protectiveness rose up in him. Chloe should know better than to keep the door unlocked. Anyone could just walk in and—

The irony wasn't lost on him but he still didn't like it.

As quietly as he could, Luke made his way into her room and set the tray on the desk. She'd been there three days but there was very little evidence of her things lying around. Luke fought the temptation to open a drawer. That was definitely crossing a line. Not that he hadn't already done that by being in her room in the first place. *Still.* He wouldn't violate her privacy any further.

Fighting the urge to go into the bathroom and deal with his craving for her once and for all, Luke turned to leave. He wasn't completely without self-control.

His hand was on the doorknob, ready to leave, when her voice stopped him.

"Luke? What the…"

He waited a breath and swallowed a curse before he turned. "I didn't mean to—" The words died on his lips when he saw Chloe, a white towel wrapped snug around her breasts; her luscious skin glistened with the water droplets that slipped down her body. Her mass of black hair was piled on her head, but a few tendrils escaped and danced around her face. Luke had to slide his hands into his back pockets to keep from reaching out and tucking the strands behind her ear.

"What are you doing in here?" she demanded. Her skin was flushed, whether from the hot water, embarrassment of being caught in a towel, or something more, Luke couldn't be sure. But it was sexy as hell.

"I was bringing you dinner." He waved in the direction of the tray. The words sounded lame even to his own ears. "You didn't answer."

"Because I was in the tub." She crossed her arms over her chest, which had the distinct benefit of pushing her tits up into the two most distracting swells Luke had ever laid eyes on. He blinked hard and refocused on her eyes, currently narrowed into slits.

She looked pissed, and there was no doubt that she was, but something else was going on, too. Even through the heavy scent of whatever floral bubble bath she'd been using, there was no mistaking the scent of desire in the air. His dick swelled in his pants at the knowledge that she assented him at least half as badly as he wanted her. He took a step toward her.

Chloe moved as if she was going to take a step backward, but she stood her ground. "You have no right to barge into my room." Her voice shook a little, but not from weakness. No. There was definitely no weakness in Chloe. It shook as if she didn't believe what she was saying. An observation Luke planned to make the most of.

"Ask me to leave." He took another step, until he was only inches from her. When she didn't immediately follow his instruction, Luke added, "If you don't want me here—want me standing here, right now—all you have to do is say the word and I'll go." He strained against his own words. The need to stay exactly where he stood was visceral.

Chloe tipped up her head. Her gorgeous blue eyes danced with indecision. Still, she said nothing.

He could feel the heat from her bath-warmed skin radiate off her. Only a short white towel stood between him and everything he wanted. Everything he needed to quell the ache growing inside him. Just once, he promised himself. That's all he'd need.

CHAPTER FIVE

He stood so close Chloe could practically feel him. He dared her with his words. If she wanted him to leave, all she had to do was say the word and this heated exchange between them would end.

She couldn't say anything. She wouldn't.

Because never in her life had Chloe wanted something—no, someone—so badly. He clouded her senses, muddled her thoughts so she couldn't make a rational decision. Logic told her she didn't want this.

But instinct told her she did. Oh, did she ever.

She swallowed hard and locked eyes with him as her internal battle raged on.

Maybe she'd been thinking of everything all wrong. She'd always thought of sex, mating, and all the mess that came with it as a life sentence. Maybe, just maybe, she needed to consider that it didn't have to be so serious. After all, what would the harm be in having a little fun? Maybe just a fling? Two consenting adults who were attracted to each other, allowing themselves to enjoy the situation without any strings?

That could work.

A smile played at her lips as she reached her decision.

She was a modern woman, and she knew what she wanted. There was no reason she couldn't have it all.

"Well?" he whispered. His breath hit her lips in short puffs. "Do you want me to go? Because if you don't answer me soon, I'm going to take it as an invitation to stay. And once I make the decision to stay, I'm not going anywhere until—"

"Until I'm done with you."

It was a bold thing to say and desire flashed in Luke's eyes at her forwardness. "Is that right?"

He still didn't touch her, but he'd moved even closer, if it was possible. Her nipples hardened, almost painfully, against the terry cloth of the towel. It would be so easy to give in and let him have his way with her. Especially considering there was no doubt the perfect specimen of a man standing before her was a far more experienced lover than she was. She wanted nothing more.

"That's right," she said, with a sassiness she didn't know she possessed. "But first, we need rules."

"Rules?" He swallowed a laugh and bent to kiss her neck.

The instant his lips touched her skin, heat exploded through her body.

She swallowed hard, determined to say what she needed to before she lost all sense of herself. "Yes, we need rules." She managed to keep her voice from shaking. Although, how she did that with his kiss moving up her neck, she couldn't be sure. "The first thing is, this is temporary. One time. That's it." As she spoke the words, Luke took her earlobe into his mouth with a gentle suction that sent sparks sizzling through her.

"One time." He murmured his agreement into her ear without pausing his ministrations. "That's all I'll need."

For what? She wanted to ask him, but it was hard enough

to focus on what she was trying to say as it was.

"Okay." Chloe nodded slightly, as Luke's hands threaded into her hair and pulled her head to the side to allow him better access. "Second rule," she continued, her breath coming in short pants now. "You have no claim on me. This is not about mating." His mouth stilled on her neck, so she added, "Ever."

For a split second, Chloe worried that it might be a deal-breaker; that stopped her for a beat because now that they'd put things into motion, she wasn't sure she could stop. But she couldn't budge on that one point. There could be no mating. No way. Luke was an itch she needed to scratch. *Period.*

After a moment that seemed to last far too long, Luke's lips moved on her body again, this time dipping lower, toward her breasts that ached for his touch. "Is that it?" he murmured against her skin.

She nodded and then, realizing he couldn't see her, breathed, "Yes."

"Good." His hands left her hair and with a quick flick, relieved her of her towel. And then his hands were on her, all over. Touching, sliding, feeling, squeezing. Everything.

They were everywhere all at once until they landed on the soft curve of her hips and lifted her easily. Normally, Chloe would feel self-conscious, but Luke stripped all that away. Chloe wrapped her legs around his waist and pressed her nakedness against him. She had such little experience with men, but she let her instincts take over. Judging by the hard mound in Luke's pants, she was doing just fine. Any thoughts of unease that might have lingered vanished when he nestled his face between her breasts, taking a moment to nuzzle them before he sucked one hard nipple into the wet heat of his mouth. He was relentless with his attentions, alternating between sucking and flicking her hard nub. Just when she thought she couldn't handle another second, he switched sides, giving both equal play before he finally lifted his head to look at her.

"You. Are. Beautiful." He dropped kisses on her chest and up her neck again until his lips finally met hers. She pulled his head closer to her, holding him to her, not wanting the kiss to end. Chloe was so lost in their connection she didn't notice him walking her to the bed, until he bent and lowered her to the mattress.

He stood over her, fully clothed, looking down at her with hunger and need all over his face. Her bear roared inside, ready to yank him back down to her if he didn't move faster. She needed him. *Now.* There was no way she could put the brakes on what was happening between them now. And that scared the hell out of her. Especially when she realized, right at the moment Luke tugged his shirt off over his head, that he'd never actually agreed to any of her rules.

Luke's animal was only barely contained as he looked at Chloe sprawled on the mattress beneath him. Her luscious, curvy body was on display for him and only him. The scent of her need for him filled the air between them. The way her lips parted, just a little, as her breath came in pants: All of it, a perfect masterpiece that made up his mate. *Chloe.* The thought caused a growl to escape his throat.

She'd made it clear she didn't want a mate, and that was fine by him. Their instincts might be leading them to each other, but they were two consenting adults; they didn't have to make it about anything more than sex. One night. That was it.

But damn, he was going to make the most of that one

night.

While she watched with heavy lids, he tossed his t-shirt to the side and slowly worked his belt through the clasp before he slid the zipper down to free his almost painfully hard erection. Her eyes widened and a noise that sounded suspiciously like a gasp escaped her lips. If he was less in tune with her, he would have let his pride swell, but there was something else in her expression. Something he couldn't ignore.

"Chloe?" He shucked his pants and crawled on to the bed, using his arms to cage her in beneath him. "Are you——"

"A virgin."

The word hung in the air between them. It was so abrupt and unexpected, Luke had to hold back from physically jumping back to give her space. He arched an eyebrow. There was no way the passionate creature beneath him was a virgin.

"Well," she corrected herself. "I'm not really a virgin. Not technically anyway, but I might as well be. I mean...I don't think a fumbling, sweaty grunting when you're sixteen really counts. I mean, I guess it does, but——"

He silenced her with a kiss. He used all his self-control to keep it soft for a moment, but it quickly escalated. He slid his tongue in her mouth, drinking up the sweetness of her, using his mouth to ease whatever tension she was feeling. He pulled back, pulling her lips with him.

"I think maybe it counts *technically*," he said. "And now I think I understand you a little bit more. But it certainly doesn't count as far as I'm concerned." He didn't give her a chance to ask for clarification before he moved backward on the bed. He used his hands to gently part her thighs before gently massaging each one while he knelt between her legs and looked up at her. Chloe's admission had taught him a lot about her. Mostly why she'd been so reluctant to give in to her very obvious, primal needs. He'd change that way of thinking. As far as he was concerned, it was a terrible travesty that her beautiful body hadn't been loved properly.

That was about to change.

He grinned mischievously and dropped his head.

"Luke, what are you—oh!"

Never in her life had Chloe allowed a man to do what Luke was doing. Not that she'd let a man do anything before. Not really. That had been her whole strategy for staying single. Now, with Luke kissing her in her most intimate place, she saw for the first time how truly wrong she'd been. She'd been missing out.

A lot.

Unsure of what to do with her hands, she reached down and threaded her hands in his hair. She could almost feel him smile against her skin as he used his tongue to lick, taste, and tease her. Chloe tipped her head back and let out a moan. Everything he was doing felt so good. Too good because before she realized it, a heat flowed through her and she could no longer contain every sensation slamming through her body. As her orgasm finally hit, Chloe arched her back and screamed out her release.

She was only vaguely aware of Luke moving over her as she allowed her body a moment to recover from what had just been the most shattering moment she'd ever experienced. When she finally opened her eyes, she looked directly into Luke's own dark eyes that watched her intently. He had a self-satisfied smirk on his face that she might have otherwise thought of as cocky, but given what he'd just done to her, that word was well deserved.

"Holy shit. That was…" were the only words she managed to get out.

"I'm not done with you yet, babe."

His words caused a shiver to run through her already sensitive body. "Good."

Luke growled and caught her mouth with his. He kissed her thoroughly as he lowered himself to her. She felt his hard length press against her. She was ready. More than ready. She was totally lost in his kiss, in the feel of him on top of her, and when he finally entered her with a hard thrust, filling her completely, it was as if they'd been born to be together.

Like mates.

Chloe pushed the thought out of her head before she could let it take root. She focused instead on every sensation firing through her body. Luke broke the kiss, lifting his head to look in her eyes. He caught each of her hands in one of his and clasped them over her head as he quickened his pace.

As Chloe's second climax built inside her, the only thing she could think of was how stupid her own rules had been. Because no matter what she'd been thinking, if this is what it was like to be with Luke, there was no way once was ever going to be enough.

CHAPTER SIX

He hadn't meant to stay the night, but after an orgasm like he'd never experienced before, there was nowhere else he wanted to be than in her bed, with Chloe in his arms. She'd been completely spent and when he'd pulled her into his chest and held her tight, with one arm around her middle to pin her close, it had only been seconds before she'd fallen into a deep sleep.

It had taken Luke a little longer to settle his brain. After what they'd experienced together, there was no way he could just close his eyes and fall asleep. Not after sex like that.

And that was the problem.

It hadn't been just sex.

It had been so much more.

Luke had never actually agreed to the silly rules she'd laid out, but on principle he agreed with them. Well, mostly with the no mating rule. They were on the same page with that one. Historically for his family, mating led to nothing but disaster. They'd been raised without his parents because of the choice of mate his mother had made. Sure, there was more to that story that nobody but their grandfather knew, but the heart of the problem was mating. Just as it was with Kira, Kade's twin. She'd also chosen a mate over her clan. Over her family. It had torn them apart, and was the entire reason Luke and his brothers were on the ridge rebuilding their lives in the first place.

No.

If mates caused such pain and drama, he wanted nothing to do with it.

It wouldn't be like that with Chloe.

The little voice in his head continually tried to chime in against all reason, but he couldn't listen. *No.* He needed to stick with his original plan: Just sex. Get her out of his system, satisfy his bear and move on. And to that end, Luke had no intention of following Chloe's other silly rule. There was no way he could keep this to *just once*. Not after discovering how explosive their connection was. That would be ridiculous.

Despite the fact that he'd just had an enormously satisfying release, just moments before, his dick swelled against her back at the thought of having her again. And that's how he'd finally drifted off, with visions of Chloe's flushed face beneath him, her hair spread on the pillowcase and that incredibly sexy noise she made when he entered her.

Which was probably why he woke in the morning with a raging erection.

At some point in the night, Chloe had rolled out of his arms. She lay on her side with her smooth, sexy, soft back facing him. He shifted on the bed, closing the slight gap between them, and lightly traced his hand down her side. His fingers trailed along her skin, exploring the dips and swells of her gorgeous body. She moaned slightly, but didn't wake.

Luke swept her hair to the side, off her shoulder, and bent his head to her exposed neck; he trailed soft kisses there while his other hand rested on her hip. With his lips, he kissed up and just under her earlobe, suckling it gently in his mouth before he whispered in her ear. "Good morning, sexy."

She stirred then, but still didn't wake, so he continued to kiss her neck; at the same time, his hand slid off her hip to the cleft between her legs. She was wet for him. Could it have been that she, too, was dreaming of him? He knew it was true. If he believed more in fated mates, he would even allow himself to think they might have had the same dreams. As it was, he wasn't going to waste time thinking of that, when there were other, more pressing issues at hand.

Slowly, his fingers moved against her sensitive nub. She moaned and shifted, opening herself to him. When Luke looked up, Chloe's eyes were open, watching him.

"Good morning, gorgeous."

She smiled and sighed again as his fingers kept moving. "Good morning," she said after a moment.

"It's about to be even better." Luke dropped his mouth to her neck again and sucked her delicate skin into his mouth, nibbling just enough to make her tremble under his touch.

"Luke…"

She didn't need to finish the thought. Luke's instincts told him everything he needed to know. He lifted her leg slightly, and moved his body in tight behind her, so he pressed against her hot opening. Chloe groaned and pushed back, right as he thrust forward, starting their day in the best possible way.

Morning sex.

Really?

Chloe still couldn't believe she'd done that. But as she let the water wash over her in the shower, she could only laugh. *Why shouldn't she have done that?* Just because she'd never allowed herself such pleasures before didn't mean she couldn't start now. Besides, it felt good. Damn good.

She allowed herself the luxury of no judgment. At least for as long as the shower lasted. After all, she'd made a deal with herself. She'd scratch the itch that was Luke. So what if they'd already broken the first rule she'd set? It was a dumb rule anyway and to be fair, she'd set that rule without realizing what she'd be giving up. Now that she knew what sex could be like, what it *was* like between them, well, no one in their right mind would limit themselves to just one time.

As for rule number two?

That one was nonnegotiable. No mates. Not now. Not ever.

She finished dressing and threw her hair in a long braid down her back. Today she needed to get outside and check out the ridge. She still had a job to do. It was important that she didn't lose sight of that. The job came first. It had to. Chloe pulled her notebook from her satchel on the desk and flipped it open to the news clipping.

Yes. The job had to come first. It might just be an environmental investigation, and to some that might not be a big deal, but it could be life-or-death. She traced her fingers over the picture of the little boy who was always forefront in her mind. She'd screwed up once before; even if it wasn't really her screw-up, she was still involved in that investigation. She'd signed off on the report that—*no*. She couldn't let those sad thoughts affect her mood this morning. But she would remember what could happen if she didn't pay attention.

That she could do.

Chloe gathered her things and took one final look in the mirror. She looked different somehow. Happier? Brighter? Whatever it was, it was evident. And it was definitely the look of a woman who'd been thoroughly satisfied.

More than once. She giggled at herself and went in search of Luke, who was going to take her out on the ridge. He only left her room little over an hour earlier, but she already looked forward to spending more time with him. Even if it was in a professional capacity.

The kitchen buzzed with activity as she pushed her way through the door. Everyone stopped and stared at her when she walked in and she didn't miss the smiles and grins on everyone's faces. Everyone but Kade, that was. He grunted and turned back to the stove. Chloe blushed like a ridiculous teenager when her eyes locked on Luke's and he gave her a wink.

"Good morning." She turned to see Harper next to her, holding a cup of coffee. The smell of it made her stomach rumble. She took the mug with a grateful smile.

"Thank you, Harper."

"No problem." The woman moved to turn away, but Chloe caught her arm.

"I was hoping to talk to you later," Chloe said. "I mean, if you're not too busy. I really wanted to apologize for—"

"There's no need." Harper's smile was sweet, but Chloe caught the glint of sadness in her eyes as well.

"Yes," she insisted. "There is. I was a jerk and I really would like the chance to make it up to you. Later? Please?"

This time Harper's smile reached her eyes when she nodded. "Okay. I'd like that."

Chloe gave the other woman an impulsive one-armed hug.

Another rumble in her stomach had Chloe looking around again, this time in search of food. "Something smells fantastic," she said.

"Pancakes." Kade grumbled and waved to a tray of perfectly golden pancakes that made Chloe's mouth water at the sight.

Before she could reach for one, Luke came up behind her, wrapped his arms around her waist and pulled her close before he whispered in her ear. "Because everyone deserves morning sex and pancakes."

She almost choked on her sip of coffee, but covered it smoothly with a laugh. She tipped her head and met his lips in a quick kiss. She should have been shy or shown even slightly more discretion, but she couldn't seem to help herself. It felt so natural to be with Luke, and he obviously didn't feel any need to hide anything from his family. Besides, it was temporary. She broke the kiss and returned to her coffee, repeating that to herself.

She had to remember that nothing long-term could ever come from whatever it was that was going on between them. They may have broken rule number one. But her second rule was going to stand. It had to.

It was a beautiful day on the ridge. The kind of day where the air was crisp enough to hint at the coming winter, but the sun shone warm enough to remind you of the hot summer days only recently enjoyed. Luke had been waiting for days to get Chloe alone out on the ridge, an excursion that promised to be even more fun now that they'd finally given in to their instincts.

At least he'd been hoping it would be more fun. For the last two hours, they'd driven in the Jeep along the rough roads. Luke had maintained a chatter about the forest, telling Chloe all he could think of about the area and how they'd gone about building the cabins and other outbuildings on the land. She'd scribbled intently in her notebook, occasionally asking questions of her own, only to scribble some more in the notebook.

Luke did his best to keep his eyes on the rough road, navigating the vehicle over the exposed roots, boulders, and ruts in the road. If he was alone, he would have just bombed through the path, absorbing the bumps and enjoying every second of it. But for Chloe's sake, he controlled himself. In more than one way. She was driving him crazy.

Even with the windows open and the fresh air flowing in, her scent filled the Jeep and his senses. He reached across the space and slid his hand onto her denim-clad thigh to give it a squeeze.

She didn't even look at him when she said, "I'm working."

Luke was about to pull away, but he saw the glint in her eyes and the way her mouth twitched up. Instead, he moved his hand up farther. She let out a soft gasp, but didn't object again so he left his hand there for a moment, deftly navigating the vehicle with his left hand.

"Shouldn't you be focusing on the road?" Chloe asked after a moment. She'd put her notebook down on her lap and watched him with a smile and a raised eyebrow.

"Baby, I'm a man of many talents."

"Oh, I'm well aware of your talents, Mr. Jackson. None of which seem to be actually providing me with a thorough tour of the property."

"Is there something else you'd like to see?" He teased her with his fingers, moving closer to the cleft between her legs.

She didn't miss a beat. "As a matter of fact, there is."

"Anything." *If she wanted to park somewhere so he could take her on a bed of pine needles, who was he to argue?*

"I need to see the property beyond the road," she said matter-of-factly. "We should get out and walk for a bit."

"Walk?" Whatever he'd been expecting her to say, that hadn't been it. "You mean, you want to go for a *run?*"

"No," she repeated. "Walk. I need to get a closer look on any environmental impact there may have been."

She was serious.

"Is there any place in particular you want to check?"

"Why don't we start farther out and work our way back to the Den? Will that work for you?"

Luke fluttered his fingers quickly against the rough denim between her legs and squeezed one more time before he returned his hand to the steering wheel. "Baby, I'll take you anywhere you want to go. All you have to do is say the word."

He wasn't making it easy for her to focus on her work, but Chloe was determined to do a good job. She'd been hired for a purpose, and despite the temptation, she would not let Luke Jackson distract her from that purpose. They could reserve their *relationship*—for lack of a better word— for the Den. But when they were out in the field, she needed to focus.

There was a reason she'd been hired to investigate. Obviously someone was worried about environmental impact and if there was something on the ridge to show that the Jackson brothers had in any way compromised the environment that they were residing in, she'd find it. Not that she wanted to find anything. But if there was anything to find, she'd make sure it was discovered. No matter what her feelings for the Jacksons were.

After Luke parked the Jeep, she hopped out and started to walk, leaving him to follow.

"You're in a hurry."

She shook her head. "I just want to do a good job."

"I can see that." There was laughter in his voice; it bristled at her but she didn't turn around. Even if he didn't take what she was doing seriously, she did. She quickened her pace. Luke had no problem catching up to her. "Hey. Wait up. How am I going to show you around if you don't wait for me?"

"I hardly need you to show me around." She spared him a glance over her shoulder. "In fact, if anything, I'd say that your presence might be a hindrance to my investigation."

He grabbed her and spun her around, catching her easily in his arms to give her a hard kiss. "My presence is anything but a hindrance to you, baby."

Her body vibrated with his touch. She hated to admit it, but he was right. There was nothing negative about his presence. Nothing at all. Chloe gave in to the kiss before she extracted herself from his embrace. "Okay," she conceded. "But I still do have to do my work. I was hired to do a job and it's important to me to do it and do it well."

"Of course it is." Luke released her and to her surprise, grabbed her hand. "And you will. So let me show you what you need to see."

Chloe tried to ignore the look on his face as he turned her and walked down the path, this time holding tightly to her hand. It was a look that went beyond the one night of passion they'd shared. Far beyond. There was much more than lust written on Luke's face.

But that wasn't what worried her.

No. The part that worried her was that whatever was going on with Luke and what he was feeling for her, Chloe just might be feeling it too. And that couldn't happen. That would ruin everything.

Chloe walked hand in hand with Luke and tried to ignore how natural it felt. Everything her cousins and sisters had ever told her about men and mates slammed into her consciousness.

It feels so good. Like you were always meant to be together. The sun is brighter, the day a little warmer…it feels like home.

Ugh.

She couldn't clear her head.

It was Luke's touch. His hand in hers *did* feel good, dammit. It wasn't supposed to. It was just supposed to be sex. And why couldn't it be? Why couldn't she just have a wild, one-night—okay, maybe more than one night—fling with a man and not have it be anything more?

Because you're a bear.

This time, her own little voice piped up.

Chloe yanked her hand out of Luke's and quickly stepped forward on the path so she walked in front of him. She had to focus and push every single one of the sickening thoughts out of her head. Including her own.

Especially her own.

To his credit, Luke didn't say a thing or question her. She thought she heard him chuckle a little, but she kept walking. She wouldn't let him get in her head. She couldn't.

"So, what is this area over here?" She purposely directed their attention to a thicket of trees next to a stream. There really was nothing of interest about the trees, but Chloe was interested in any distraction at all. Anything to get her focus off the incredibly sexy man whose presence behind her had her body on high alert.

"I'm glad you asked."

She stopped and turned in surprise, almost running into his hard chest. A fate that wouldn't have been so bad at all.

No. She must stop thinking like that.

Chloe cleared her throat. "Why?"

Luke grabbed her hand and charged off the trail, dragging her along with him toward the stream. "Because this is one of my favorite fishing holes."

Chloe looked up and down at the tiny, shallow stream. "It hardly looks like a fishing *hole*. There's no way fish can live in here. It's too shallow."

"No way." Luke laughed and without letting go of her hand, stepped nimbly along the rocks that bordered the stream, taking her up with him. "Please don't tell me you've never been fly fishing before."

"Okay. I won't tell you."

His face twisted into an expression that resembled something between humor and disappointment. "I don't mean this to sound, well, abrupt...but...you're a bear. How have you never been fishing before?"

"I'm a girl."

"I noticed." He wiggled his eyebrows at her and Chloe had to bite back a laugh. "What difference does that make?"

Chloe stared down into the crystal-clear waters that gently flowed past her feet and shrugged. "It's just the way things were done in my clan. The men provided and the women...we mated." It was kind of a sore spot with Chloe, but Luke didn't need to know that. There had been a lot of chauvinistic tendencies in the Karrington clan, which was one of the reasons she'd left. Besides, she was over it. Mostly.

"That's stupid." Luke stated it so matter-of-factly that Chloe looked up. He watched her with a strange gaze. "We grew up as the grandchildren of a very dominating alpha of the clan. And when I say very dominating, well…I mean just that. But even then, we used to take my little sister fishing all the time. We taught her to do everything we did. And frankly, a lot of the time she did it better than us. But don't tell Kira." His eyes lit up when he spoke of his sister.

"I haven't met her." Chloe suddenly wanted very much to meet Kira. "Does she help out at the Den, too?"

The shadow that fell over Luke's fast was instant. He shook his head and looked away. "No. We don't see Kira anymore." It was clear from his tone that the subject was a hard one. Chloe paused for a moment, watching Luke for a sign that it might be okay. When the set line of his mouth didn't change, Chloe changed the subject.

"What kind of fish do you catch here?"

It took Luke a moment to shake off the earlier conversation, but it seemed that talking about fish was the way to do it. "Trout. Bull trout mainly. But sometimes you can get a rainbow or two once in a while. And of course it depends on the fly I use. Fly fishing is more of an art than a sport. It's incredible, really."

It didn't take long for Luke's face to lose the shadows of a past that clearly haunted him and once again light up as he spoke about fishing. Although Chloe had never had much of an interest in fishing beyond wanting to show up her male relatives, she couldn't help getting pulled into the world that Luke created while he spoke of flies, fish, and casting.

Luke had never before found anyone who listened to him about fishing the way Chloe was doing. Maybe his brothers, but even then their interest was limited to finding out what they could to beat him at his own game. Luke had always been the best fisherman in the family. It was a role he was proud of because it was about so much more than just simply catching fish. It was about timing and strategy and patience. Qualities and traits that his brothers didn't necessarily have. More than that, he'd never before had the opportunity to talk about his passion so openly to someone who seemed to care so deeply.

And Chloe cared.

Even if she didn't understand all of what he said, she was definitely listening. And that meant the world to him. This woman, she was so much more than a gorgeous, curvy bear. She was smart, sexy, more sensual than even she knew, and his perfect match in every way.

His mate.

He hated even thinking the word, but there was no other word to describe it. He'd been fighting it. From the moment he'd met her, he'd been fighting it. But there was no way he could deny it. Luke could tell himself whatever he wanted to about why it was no good to get mixed up with a mate and why he should probably be running for the hills. But no matter what he told himself, the reality was he couldn't bring himself to send her away or shut her off. It was the total opposite. The more time he spent with her, the more he wanted to wrap her in his arms, hold her, kiss her, and tell her how much he needed her in his life.

And that scared the hell out of him.

He risked a quick glance in Chloe's direction as he talked to her about casting into a pool where he knew for a fact there would be bull trout hiding. Her black hair shone in the sunlight, begging to be let out of the tight braid she had it tied back in. Luke wanted to let it free, have it cascade over her shoulders so he could twine his fingers through the strands and pull her face down to his so he could kiss her until she begged him for more. Because she would. Of that he had no doubt. He spotted a private area under a pine that looked soft enough for a makeshift bed, where he could take her and have her every which way they desired. And that was saying something.

Luke forced himself to focus and keep it clean. She was working and she'd made it very clear that her work was important to her; he wouldn't take that away from her or compromise it in any way.

With some effort, he concentrated on the pool they were watching. "The bull trout like to hide at the bottom," he said. "If you look really closely, you might even see one hiding along the edges of the rock. They watch and wait."

Her eyes were focused on the water. "What are they waiting for?"

He shrugged. "The right fly to come along. Sometimes they can be tricky buggers. But if I want one bad enough, I'll get him."

Chloe looked up at him with a smirk. "Confident, aren't you?" She popped her hip out and he was positive she didn't have the slightest idea of how sexy it made her at that moment.

"Absolutely." Luke licked his bottom lip and took a step around the pool toward her. "Baby, when I want something, I always get it."

He grabbed her by the waist and pulled her close. *Work be damned.* He could no longer resist her.

"You think so, do you?" She teased him with her question, but it was a challenge Luke wasn't going to back down from.

He closed the slight distance between them so her mouth was only inches from his. "I don't *think* anything," he said, slowly. "When it comes to fishing, I always make my catch." He crushed her lips to his and slid one hand down her back to her ass, where he held her firmly against him. He wasn't going to let her go. There was no way. It only took seconds for any resistance she was holding onto to melt away. Her kiss in return was hard and fueled by the passion he knew she felt for him. This woman was absolutely everything.

He hated on so many levels to admit it. But the taste of her, the feel of her—damn, the *scent* of her—made his entire body come alive. And now that he had her, he couldn't let her go. He wouldn't.

After a moment, Chloe eased off the kiss. He could feel the staccato rise and fall of her chest against his. There was absolutely no doubt what kind of effect he had on her: the same one she had on him. She pulled back, just enough so he could look into her eyes. The emotion churning in those blue depths reminded him of the way the stream frothed over the stones into his favorite fishing hole. There was a lot more going on beneath the surface than Chloe let on.

She licked her lips. Luke swallowed hard. She opened her mouth to say something, and instinctively, Luke knew he wasn't going to want to hear it. She was fighting their connection so hard. She might as well be physically pushing him away. But she wasn't. His grip on her tightened. *Not yet.*

"Before you say anything," he cut her off before a word came out of her mouth. "I want to tell you something."

Chloe closed her mouth, and looked at him with an *okay I'll humor you for a moment* look on her face. Her body tensed in his arms as if she was ready to run, but he wasn't about to let her go. Not yet.

Maybe not ever.

"I know you don't want this," he started. "Or maybe I should say that you *think* you don't want this." Chloe opened her mouth again, but Luke silenced her with a gentle finger to her lips. "But you do. I can feel how much you want this."

Chloe laughed then, but it wasn't a cute sound, or a happy noise. It was forced, tense, scared almost, as if she'd just discovered she'd left the house without pants.

"I know you do, Chloe," he continued, ignoring the noise. "I can feel it. I can *sense* it. Because it's not just you. It's me, too." She squeezed her eyes and looked away, but Luke was not about to be deterred. "And don't think for a second that falling for you was something I wanted either."

That got her attention. She whipped her head around. "*Falling* for me? You barely know me. You know—"

"Everything I need to." He stared into her eyes hard, forcing her to meet his gaze. "I know that you were made for me. When I'm with you, my bear is finally satiated, calm. When I'm inside you, well...we fit. And you know it." She blinked hard but didn't look away. "I know you feel it too, Chloe. I've tried to fight it. Hell, do you really think I want to mess up my life with a mate? I've been doing just fine without any—"

"A mate?" Her eyebrows arched into dangerous peaks. "Who said anything about a *mate?*"

"Don't fight it."

She squirmed in his grasp. "I think I'll do just that, thank you very much."

"You can't." Despite the fact that his mate was fighting him on every level, Luke had never felt calmer. He wasn't worried. It might take a little convincing, but as soon as she let down her walls a little, he had no doubt she'd see what Luke already knew. *They were fated.*

"Look, Chloe." He tightened his grip on her, but used his thumbs to stroke soft circles on her upper arms. "It's not what I had planned for myself either. I get it. But just like with Axel and Harper, it's—"

"It's bullshit."

Chloe twisted hard to the left and escaped his hands, scooting herself out of reach. He could easily close the gap and hold her again, but he'd give her space. If she needed a bit of time to come to the same conclusion he had, that's what she needed. He wasn't worried.

"You're fairly sure of yourself." Chloe adjusted her shirt but she wouldn't meet his eye, which only affirmed exactly why he should be so sure of himself. "I told you, I'm not interested in anything. I shouldn't even have done what...well, we shouldn't have."

"Oh yes we should have." Luke jumped over the rocks that separated them, and twined his arm around her waist, pointing into the stream below them as he did. "Just like those fish—once you cast with just the right fly, they have no choice but to take the bait."

Chloe made an adorable sound halfway between a chuckle and a snort but she covered her mouth so quickly, Luke was robbed of the chance to see her beautiful lips in a smile. "Did you just compare me to a *trout*?"

"I did."

"And you think you're going to be able to reel me in, do you?"

He took another step closer and closed the gap. "I think I have just the bait you need."

There was no way he could stand so close to her, breathing in the fresh, rich scent of her and not pull her into his arms, so that's just what he did. "You know we could save a whole lot more time if you didn't keep running away from me." Luke didn't wait for a reply before he took that sexy mouth into a kiss, leaving no doubt in anyone's mind what exactly they could be doing with all that saved time.

He was happy to take her right there next to his favorite fishing hole, under the pines in a bed of needles. In fact, he couldn't think of a better place to finally make her his mate, not that she was ready to agree to that. Yet. When Chloe stiffened in his arms once more, it took all Luke's self-control not to roar out in frustration. When she pulled away from his kiss, he had to swallow hard to keep his bear in check. He opened his eyes to see her staring over his shoulder at something behind him. Judging by the storm swirling in her blue depths, he wasn't going to like what he saw when he turned around.

"What the hell is that?" She left him standing behind her, ignoring the question on his lips, in his eyes. She needed space from him in order to think. She'd been clouded. *Way* too clouded. Luke had a way of getting up into her senses and distracting her from everything she needed to focus on.

No more.

Especially now.

Chloe picked her way across the slick stones in the stream and climbed up the bank into the woods to investigate what had caught her eye.

It hadn't looked like much from the stream. But it had looked as if it might not belong in the forest. Chloe didn't want it to be anything. She hoped it was nothing, but the closer she got to the flash of color that had caught her eye, the clearer it became that it was indeed something.

Something that was definitely not going to be a good thing for Grizzly Ridge or Luke and his brothers.

She kicked at the piece of green plastic that stuck out from the branches. Where it had been obviously covered up. And not well. Chloe grabbed a stick and used it to uncover the rest.

Her heart skipped, and not in the good, heart fluttering way it had skipped earlier when she'd been in Luke's arms. This was more of a *crap-this-is going-to-change-everything and not in a good way* type of flutter.

"What the hell is that?" She didn't turn around, but could feel Luke's strong presence directly behind her. She hated to admit it, but her body thrilled with the proximity.

She forced herself to focus. "It looks like garbage to me, Luke. An unlawful dumping ground if I ever saw one." She pushed herself up, careful not to bump into Luke, who was still so close, and walked farther into the woods, following the trail that clearly looked as if it led to more garbage.

"This is bullshit." Luke followed her, kicking at the ground as he went. "This isn't ours. We didn't put it here."

Chloe ignored him and pulled her camera out of her side bag.

"Don't take pictures." She dodged to the side as Luke lunged for her camera. "This is bullshit. I told you we didn't put it here."

"Luke, I have to." Chloe forced herself to stay calm in the face of Luke's growing anger. "It's my job."

"No." His face was twisted in a snarl. "Your job is to investigate the truth."

She stood her ground, her chin lifted in the air, her hands firmly on her camera, her heart throbbing with loss.

"Luke." She spoke slowly but decisively so there would be no confusion. "The truth is, there is garbage here and it's your land. My job is to investigate that connection."

"There's no goddamn connection, Chloe. We didn't put it here. It's not ours." His words were a snarl, and it wasn't hard to see his animal was only just barely contained. She had plenty of experience with alpha types before, and Chloe knew enough to tread lightly. The only problem was knowing and doing were two very different things.

"We'll have to see," she said.

It was the wrong thing to say. Luke let out a roar that shook the trees around them and vibrated in her chest.

Resolutely, she ignored him and once again pointed her camera at the evidence. She snapped a few pictures before he could try to grab her camera again and tucked it back in her bag. Chloe could hear him grumble and curse behind her, but she still didn't turn to look at him. Nothing about what she was seeing made sense. Everything she'd already seen at Grizzly Ridge and with the Jackson brothers spoke to environmental consciousness of the highest level, but she couldn't ignore what she was seeing. She just couldn't. It was her job to investigate, and that meant that whatever she felt for Luke had to be put aside. Especially considering she wasn't even sure what she felt for Luke.

First things first. Chloe crouched down in front of one of the mounds. Using her stick, she poked through the pile.

"There's nothing to *see*, Chloe."

She ignored him again.

"Chloe."

Her heart ached as his voice twisted her name. It was only moments before he'd said her name with something akin to love in his voice. That was gone.

She swallowed hard. "I'm sorry, Luke. I am. But—"

"Then you're on your own."

She turned around then, just in time to see him stalk off toward where they'd parked the Jeep. Her first instinct was to run after him. To stop him from leaving her in the forest. But there was no point. He needed space. He was clearly upset and she couldn't blame him. She was just as upset, but she still had a job to do. And the reality was, Chloe knew all too well what could happen if she didn't do it properly.

CHAPTER SEVEN

"Axel!" The heavy wooden door hit the wall behind it and Luke stormed into the Den. He should care about their guests hearing him. He should care about maintaining a sense of decorum. He should care about Chloe stranded in the woods.

He didn't.

All he cared about was finding out who the hell was responsible for the garbage in the woods. In *his* woods.

"Axel?" He bellowed again, and when the two ladies on the couch in front of the fireplace jumped up, Luke didn't even flinch. His brother was either in his office or in the kitchen; either way, he'd better make his presence known, and soon.

"Axel, where the hell—"

The swinging door to the kitchen flew open; Kade stood there, a small white apron around his waist and a towel in his hand. "Luke? Why don't you come in here?" He bit off each word as if it were jerky, leaving no room for question.

Luke stalked past him into the kitchen. The moment the door shut behind him, he turned. "Where the hell is Axel? We need to talk. Now."

"What's going on?"

Luke whirled to see Axel and Harper walk into the kitchen through the back door. They looked happy and glowing in that way they always seemed to be lately. That way that screamed of new love, or mated love, or whatever it was that Axel insisted it

70

was. The fact that less than an hour ago Luke felt the exact same way about Chloe didn't register. He had bigger things to worry about and maybe if Axel hadn't been so damn preoccupied with a female, he wouldn't have to be bringing it to his attention now. When it was probably too late.

Luke flashed back to the image of Chloe crouched down in front of a pile of garbage on his land. By his favorite fishing hole, no less. The look on her face. The utter disgust that he could be part of something so dirty.

He wasn't.

But someone was.

He looked at both his brothers in turn. "Who dumped garbage by the stream?"

"What?" Kade choked as he took a sip from a water bottle. He wiped his mouth with the back of his arm and put the bottle down. "What are you talking about?"

"Garbage," Luke said again. He looked to Axel this time, who watched Luke very carefully. He didn't say a word to either confirm or deny anything, but his eyes narrowed as Luke continued. "Chloe and I were walking out by the ridge today. I took her by the stream. Showed her where I was going to lead some fishing groups and we—"

"Chloe?"

"Of course Chloe," Luke spat at Harper. He immediately felt guilty, but he didn't apologize. "She needed to see the land in order to complete her—"

"Where is she now?"

Harper glared at him and crossed her arms over her chest. She was definitely not a female to be messed with. She'd never accepted his attitude, and he couldn't imagine she was about to start now.

"Luke?" Axel said carefully. "Harper asked you where Chloe was."

He looked carefully between his brothers and Harper, meeting each of their eyes in turn. They clearly knew something was up, but they were missing the point completely. "She's fine. You guys need to focus." He tried to bring them back to the issue at hand. "There's garbage on the ridge and I need to know who put it there."

"Right," Axel said. "And since you're not saying anything, I assume that's where Chloe is."

"Dammit, Luke." With a hard yank, Kade tugged his apron off and tossed it on the counter. "I'll go get her."

"She's fine." The words came out as a growl. Both protective and threatening at the same time. The combination only confused him further. He was so angry with his mate for not believing him, for not giving him the benefit of the doubt, but at the end of the day, she was still that. *His mate.*

"It's going to get dark soon," Axel said calmly and tossed Kade some keys. "Take the truck. It sounds like she'll have something to bring back."

He wanted to stop his little brother, but even through his rage, Luke could see it was the right thing to do and let him go. He shouldn't have left her there. And he wouldn't have if he hadn't known she'd be fine on her own. She was a bear, for God's sake; the woman knew just as well as him how to survive on her own. And if anyone tried to sneak up on her or harm her, well…he felt sorry for whoever was stupid enough to do that. Especially because when Chloe was done with them, he'd have a turn as well. The fierce protectiveness reared up in him again. It was completely at odds with everything he felt for her and he shoved it aside to focus on the real issue.

"I found garbage up by Cooper's Creek. The hole where the bull trout are. Who put it there?"

"Garbage?"

"Garbage." Luke's patience was being stretched like a stale rubber band. If he didn't get some answers soon it wasn't going to be pretty. "It looked to be more than one pile, too. Like it had been dumped for a while." Even as he explained it, something about it didn't ring true.

"Luke." Harper stepped between the two brothers. "What makes you think for a second that we would know anything about any garbage anywhere on the ridge? Let alone by the creek? You can't seriously be standing here thinking we know something about it?"

He looked to his brother. *No.* Axel loved the ridge just as much as he did. Maybe more. And despite all his attitude lately, Kade did too. It wasn't them. There was no way. But someone knew something. Someone was responsible for the garbage. And more importantly, someone was responsible for the way Chloe had looked at him. His eyes locked on Harper.

She immediately recoiled at his glare and Axel wrapped his arm around her. No doubt less to defend her and more to protect Luke. "You can't be serious?" She shook her head, not in anger but almost in pity, likely for the complete and total disaster of emotions he'd become in less than a week. "You know better, Luke." She waited a beat. "You *know* better."

He shrugged and muttered an apology. He *did* know better.

"Alright." Axel moved across the large kitchen to the fridge and grabbed two beers from their private stock. He threw one to Luke, but before cracking his own, he quickly prepped a tray with a bottle of wine and a few glasses and handed it to Harper, who already seemed to know what his intentions were.

"I'll go make sure the guests weren't too rattled by Luke's outburst." She shot Luke a look but softened it by blowing him a kiss before she pushed out into the main room to tend to their guests. The second she was gone, Axel started in on him.

"Are you kidding me, Luke? What the hell was that all about? You really think you can stand here and accuse Harper or any of us, for that matter, of dumping garbage by the stream? Are you crazy? Or drunk? Or...never mind."

"What?" Luke took a deep drink of his beer. "What were you going to say?"

Axel shook his head as if his little brother wasn't worth whatever comment he was going to make, but Luke wasn't stupid; he knew exactly what he was going to say. It was the exact same thing he would have, and in fact, did say, to him not all that long ago when Axel's head was muddled by the presence of his mate before he claimed her. *His instincts were clouded because of Chloe.* He knew it and it made him crazy. But there wasn't anything he could do about that particular problem. At least not for now. He needed to focus.

One thing at a time.

And right now, the most important thing was to figure out who'd put the garbage on their land. Before Chloe did.

"You know what? It doesn't matter." Luke waved away whatever Axel was going to say and finished the rest of his beer in one big swallow. "Right now there's only one thing that matters. Who would have done this?"

"It has to be someone with access to the ridge. If it's by Cooper's Creek, that's not an easy place to get to, but—"

"It's a place that would be—"

"Discovered."

They locked eyes and nodded. "Exactly," Luke said. "But who would have a reason to—"

"The wolves."

"Blackwood."

The brothers spoke at the same time. "Dammit." Luke's fist came down hard on the countertop, rattling the dishes. "I should have known. I should have known from the moment Chloe showed up here talking about *environmental impact* and all that bullshit. She's working for the wolves."

"Whoa." Axel got in front of him and placed both hands on his chest, stopping his pacing. "You don't know that."

"I *do* know that. She said she was hired by an outside party. A *concerned* party. Who would that be? Who would really be so concerned about our business except for the only group who might have something to lose by it?"

"The wolves don't have a damn thing to lose by us being here. We've done nothing but work together with them. Our weakness is their strength and vice versa."

"Do they see it that way?" Luke's eyes challenged his brother and he held them until finally he saw the flicker of doubt reflected back at him. "Right," he said. "I think it's time to find out."

Chloe should have been furious. She should have been out for blood. She should have been a lot of things when it came to Luke Jackson and the way he'd just abandoned her in the middle of the forest. But all she really was was sad.

Sure, she'd been fighting their attraction. But fighting it or not, she wasn't blind. She wasn't completely ignorant to the way her body thrilled when he was near. The way her bear came alive. The way everything suddenly felt so damn right.

But none of that mattered anymore. She could not ignore what she'd seen in the forest. She had to investigate whether Luke liked it or not, and judging by his reaction earlier, he wasn't going to like it. Not at all.

It didn't matter. It couldn't matter. Something was going on at the ridge. Something that shouldn't be.

It couldn't be Luke.

The little voice in her head, the same little voice that had made itself known since she'd discovered the trash, spoke up again. It would not be quieted. Chloe shook her head, ignoring it. *One thing at a time.* The first thing she needed to do was sift through the garbage and see whether she could find some sort of indication of where it came from.

Kade had set her up in a sheltered picnic area behind the Den. It was open on one side, but the walls should protect from any breeze that might come up and the weather was forecasted to be okay for next few days. It wasn't ideal, but it would do.

Of course, as well as setting her up in the shed, Kade had also done quite a bit of apologizing for his brother abandoning her in the middle of the forest as he drove her back to the main building. She'd only shrugged and tried to pretend it didn't bother her. But it did. Not because she couldn't figure out how to get back; she was a bear, for God's sake—of course she could figure out how to get back to the Den. *No.* It bothered her on a much deeper level.

He'd left her. Just when she was starting to believe that maybe, just maybe she could actually believe in the whole mated for life thing—and more importantly, that she could make it work, that she *wanted* to make it work—he went and left her.

And didn't that just affirm everything?

She'd definitely have to be more guarded from now on. If he was the type of man who would throw her aside because she had to do her job, Luke Jackson was definitely not the right man for her. Assuming she wanted a man at all.

She groaned out loud and wiped her hair off her forehead with the back of her gloved hand. "Focus, Chloe. The only thing you need to do right now is focus on this job. It's important."

"Is it?"

Chloe whirled around at the voice and scattered some of the garbage off the table. She left it for the moment because she couldn't take her eyes off Luke's. He looked pained, haunted, and something else. Something much more frightening.

"What?" Chloe stumbled over the word, unsure of what she was even asking.

Luke took a step closer to her. He didn't look at the piles of garbage, the evidence that only hours ago had him roaring in anger. Instead, he kept his eyes locked on hers. Intense. Focused. A shiver ran through her, and she locked her arms around herself and squeezed to keep from trembling.

"Is it important?" he asked again as he took another step. "Is it really?"

She nodded and kept her chin set high. *She would not let him get to her. She would not let him distract her from her job.* "It is. It's very important. Anytime the environment is threatened, we need to take it very seriously. It's my job."

"I understand that." He was close now. *Really close. Too close.* "What I meant was, is it the garbage that's really important or finding out who put it there what really matters?"

"Both." Chloe took a step back and to the side, focusing on the pile in front of her. It was the perfect distraction from Luke and more specifically, how his presence made her entire body come alive. It was definitely best to put a table of trash between them. "By looking through the evidence, it should be pretty clear who dumped it and then from there we can move forward to discovering things like why and when. And once we've determined that...charges."

"Charges?"

Chloe looked up. "Of course. There will definitely be charges laid. And they're serious ones. People need to be held accountable for this type of behavior. The fines are steep and sometimes result in jail time, or at the very least will make a strong financial impact on the guilty party."

"You make it sound serious."

Her eyes narrowed and she had to bite back a response. She'd dealt with this type of attitude before. People didn't think of environmental impact as serious. But it was. And monitoring it, and when necessary, stopping the damage could sometimes even be life-or-death. Jordan's face flashed in her mind the way it always did when she was working a case. She may have let him down, but never again.

"Dumping is illegal," she continued. "And while it looks like this particular site was fairly contained, it's usually indicative of another site nearby. Typically, it's not a one-time thing. Another site may have more toxicity or pollutants that could potentially damage the ecosystem further and in some cases, the water supply or the health of the residents."

"There is no other site."

She tipped her head and crossed her arms again, waiting for him to elaborate.

"It was the wolves."

"The wolves?"

"They run Blackwood Ranch down in the valley."

"And you think it was the Blackstones who dumped the garbage?" She refused to refer to them by anything but their last name.

"It had to be them. We wouldn't have done it. We love our land too much. It's everything to us, Chloe." He locked eyes on hers again; his words implied more than he said. She got the message loud and clear: the land was everything to him. Not a woman, not a potential mate. *Not her.*

She cleared her throat and, using the tongs she'd borrowed from the kitchen, sifted through the first bag. "I guess the evidence will tell us what we need to know then."

Chloe didn't look up, but she knew he hadn't left. She could sense him standing there, watching her. Resolutely, she ignored him and continued to work. Most of the first bag was kitchen garbage. She had to focus on breathing through her mouth, to keep from inhaling the putrid scent. Coffee grounds, egg shells, and potato peels. "At the very least, this person could learn how to compost," she snorted under her breath.

"Kade started a composting bin this last summer. The plan is to use it for a garden in the spring. So there you go—it's not us."

Still, she didn't look up. "It's not that simple." She swept the kitchen garbage aside and moved to the next bag. The moment she sliced through the plastic, she knew this bag would be more telling. It was full of paper. The first piece she picked up had a familiar blue logo on the top and the words, "Grizzly Ridge."

She looked up slowly and shook her head. She didn't want it to be true. She'd been holding out, assuming it wasn't true. Assuming that there was no way Luke or his brothers could be part of something like garbage dumping. *No way. It couldn't be...*

"What the hell?" Luke snatched the paper from her hands and she let him have it because there was more, a lot more in the bag that sat in front of her. "This isn't what it looks like."

"It looks like your letterhead." She couldn't meet his eyes.

"I know what it *looks* like." He shook the paper. "But it isn't ours."

Chloe shook her head and bent to the task in front of her. If she looked up, she knew exactly what she'd see and she couldn't bear it.

"Don't shake your head, Chloe. Don't look like that." His voice grew more panicked, frantic, heated, but still, she couldn't look up. "Don't you dare ignore me—and take that look of pity off your face! This isn't us, Chloe."

She did look up then. "Luke, I'm sorry."

He moved so quickly, she didn't have time to react. Luke was around the picnic table, his hands on her face in a tender cradle that belied the anger and frustration she could feel flowing through him. "Chloe." Her name on his lips was heartbreaking as he pleaded for her to listen, to understand. But that was exactly what she was trying to do. "You can't really believe this is us." His voice was barely more than a whisper. "You can't believe this is *me*."

"I...I'm—"

He swallowed her words in a kiss unlike she'd ever had before. They'd shared passion, but this was different. It was heated. Packed with emotion. Infused with a different type of need.

Chloe groaned into his mouth as her body betrayed her and came alive. He walked backward with her and pressed her against the rough wooden wall, pinning her under him. She should put a stop to it. She should push him away and finish her work. But when his hands slipped down her body to her waist and the button on her pants, the ache that had been building inside her intensified. She shucked the gloves from her hands and captured his head in her hands, forcing him to look at her.

"I need you." The words were rough, raw. And she knew exactly what he meant, because she, too, needed him in a way unlike any she'd ever felt before. He pushed her pants down, moving to his own belt buckle, all the while holding her with his dark eyes, an unasked question there.

She nodded, giving him the permission he was seeking. A low growl escaped him and she matched it with her own as he lifted her easily and entered her in one solid stroke. Chloe bit her bottom lip to control the emotion crashing through her.

There was no doubt in her mind that she was fated to Luke. He was her mate, he was her everything, and knowing that should have made everything better. It should have quelled the storm inside her, but it only added to the chaos in her heart. As they rode out their passion together in a hard, frenzied need, instead of feeling like home, it felt like good-bye. Because nothing could ever be the same again.

CHAPTER EIGHT

Dawn had barely broken over the ridge when Luke left his cabin and slammed the door behind him. The night had been long. Too long without Chloe by his side. But he couldn't have her again. Not the way he needed her. Next to him, curled up into him, that soft, round ass pressed into his—

No. It was best to not even think about her. That was done. They'd said their good-bye in the shed, right there in front of the *evidence* that she planned to ruin him with. And she did plan on that; he knew it. He also knew she had a job to do and she thought she was doing it. Never mind that the garbage wasn't theirs. It *looked* like theirs. He couldn't blame her for that. He couldn't stop her from doing her job.

No matter how much he wanted to.

It was too important to her. Heck, it was part of who she was. Part of the woman he loved.

And that's why he'd said good-bye. Not in so many words, of course, but they both knew what that last coupling had meant. He'd felt the intensity from her just as surely as she'd felt it from him. They couldn't happen. They couldn't be. Fated mates or not, it wasn't happening.

And they both knew it.

Unless he could figure something else out. And that's just what he planned to do.

He didn't have proof yet, but in his heart, Luke knew that all of this had started with the wolves and by the time he was finished with them, it was going to end with the wolves.

No time for breakfast, or more importantly, having anyone stop him, Luke bypassed the Den and headed straight for his truck. Confronting the Blackwoods needed to be something he did on his own. It was true that they hadn't been thrilled that Luke and his brothers had set up on the Ridge, positioning themselves as the first eco-tourism lodge in Montana, but the Jacksons weren't competing for the Blackwoods' business. They'd been a working ranch for decades and in the last ten years or so had added the tourism aspect and offered dude ranch experiences. That was not at all what the Jacksons were doing. They specialized in hikes and mountain biking, and soon…fishing. In fact, Luke often arranged trail rides for their guests down at Blackwood Ranch. They'd been nothing but reasonable. If the wolves had a problem with them, sabotage was definitely not the way to deal with it. That would become very clear. Very soon.

Once he was in the truck, he didn't bother to be quiet as he roared out of the drive and down the gravel road. No doubt Axel had heard him fire up the engine and was probably pacing at that very moment. He'd know exactly what Luke was up to. Although his older brother would no doubt like to take a more diplomatic approach to things with their neighbors, Luke was pretty sure the time for that was over.

It was time for action.

Just as he'd expected it to be, the ranch was already

awake. People moved about, mostly by the barns, getting the horses ready for the day's events. But the barns weren't where Luke was headed. Brian Blackwood was bound to be in his office, and that's exactly where he was going. He parked the truck right out in front of the main building, not concerned whether anyone saw him or not, and stormed through the front doors.

Luke had only been in the main ranch building once or twice before, but it wasn't hard to find the small hallway where the offices were located. Conveniently, Brian's was marked by a slice of wood on the front. Forgoing the knock, Luke tried the handle.

"Blackwood. We need to talk."

The other man looked up from his work and ran a hand through his shaggy head of hair. If he was surprised to see Luke, he didn't show it. Instead, he smiled his wolfish grin and stood. He was shorter than Luke, but still a solid man. In a fistfight, it would be an evenly paired match. Despite his itch to hit something, or someone, Luke didn't want it to come to blows.

"Luke." He nodded. "What brings you to the ranch this morning? Looking for a trail ride? I have a nice calm mare that would be perfect for you. Real gentle."

"Cut the shit, Blackwood. I'm not in the mood."

The humor melted from the other man's face and he straightened. "I see that. What's up?"

"I thought we were good." Luke waved a hand between them. "You and I," he clarified. "I thought the Jacksons and the Blackwoods were working pretty well out here. No fights, no feuds. That changes. Today."

Brian's face changed instantly; any traces of laughter and teasing were gone, replaced only by confusion and a good dose of wariness. Even to a wolf, a bear throwing down a challenge was nothing to be messed with. "We are good," he said. "Whatever you think is the problem is just that—you thinking it. We have no issue with you."

"Really?" Luke could feel his bear roar inside him, eager to get out and run or fight. Whatever would take the edge off fastest. "Then explain the garbage," he said. "And the woman." He swallowed back the sour taste in his mouth, referring to Chloe so casually, but it wouldn't do any good to let his potential enemy know that Chloe was his mate.

"You're talking crazy." Brian shook his head with a snort of laughter and moved to sit down again. "I don't know anything about any garbage, and I know even less about a woman. Although, if you're worked up about her, she's probably worth—"

Luke moved around the desk so quickly, Brian didn't see it coming. He slammed Brian up against the wall and pinned him with one hand on his shoulder, his other coiled in a fist. "Don't say one more word."

Anger flashed in Brian's green eyes; his lips lifted to reveal his canines and a low growl started in his chest, but he made no move to get free. "So clearly she's important to you," he said simply. "But I still have no idea what you're talking about. Now if you're done with your caveman act for the moment, we can figure out exactly what the hell you're talking about because I think it's obvious it's a problem."

The other man's calm tone soaked through Luke's anger, and after another deep breath, he let go of Brian and backed off. "Sorry," he grumbled. They may not be best buddies, but even as clouded as his instincts were at the moment, even Luke could see Brian didn't know anything. If he had, he would have fought back and neither of them would be standing there as whole as they were. "But someone knows something, and I need to—"

"You need to figure it out." Brian straightened his shirt

and gestured for Luke to take a seat before he pulled his own chair up to sit. "Tell me what's going on and I'm sure if we work together, we can come to some sort of solution. What's this about garbage?" Brian winked at him. "And more importantly, tell me about the woman."

"You look like you could use some more coffee."

Chloe looked up from the table where she'd been cradling her head and half sleeping, half thinking, but mostly just daydreaming and looked up at Harper. She gratefully took the fresh mug of coffee the other woman offered her, pushing aside the one already in front of her. The one that had grown cold because she'd been too busy feeling sorry for herself.

"Thank you." She forced a smile, but there was no way it came close to reaching her eyes. Even if she had been able to get a solid night's sleep, Chloe was pretty sure she couldn't have found much to smile about.

"Wanna talk about it?" Harper slid into the seat across from her without waiting for an invitation.

Chloe blinked hard and took a sip of the hot coffee. This woman was so unwaveringly kind to her, and Chloe had been nothing but a bitch. She shook her head in response to her own thoughts, but Harper took it as an answer.

"It's okay," she said. "You don't have to talk if you don't want to. But I do know that sometimes, it can really help. I mean, I don't know everything that's going on and something tells me it's a lot more than even you know, but I do know about the whole mating part."

Chloe shook her head, hard. And almost spat out her coffee. "Oh no. You've got it wrong. I'm not...we're not…I mean, it's not like that."

Harper lifted her mug, but it didn't hide her knowing smile. "Sure it's not."

"It's not." Chloe put the mug down with so much force, it sloshed over the side. "I mean, it's really not. We fooled around, yes. But…" *Why was she even telling Harper that?* Not that it was a secret, but still. Some things should be private. But she couldn't seem to stop herself. "It's not like we're mates. We're not. It's totally not like that." She picked up her mug again, trying for cool, calm, and collected. All things she failed miserably at.

"I'm not going to push, Chloe. But I am going to tell you that I know what it's like to feel like you're out of control and that something is happening *to* you. That's part of what this mating thing is all about. And think about it from my perspective for a minute. I didn't even know I was a bear. Can you imagine? I thought I was just going crazy." Harper laughed and the sound was so real and so genuine, it put her at ease.

"That *would* complicate things." She rolled the mug between her hands, letting the warmth fill her. "I certainly don't have to worry about that."

"No." Harper bent her head in an effort to catch Chloe's eye. "But you do have to worry about other things. Like your job."

Just the mention of it sent Chloe's stomach roiling again.

"My point is, it never seems to be easy, Chloe. Why don't you let me help you talk it out?"

This time it was an offer she couldn't refuse, because what was the point? She took another sip of her coffee, letting the black liquid fortify her and told Harper her story, starting at the very beginning, with her childhood and her need for independence.

Harper listened in silence and when Chloe finally paused, she nodded thoughtfully. "So what makes you think you can't have it all?"

It wasn't the question Chloe expected. "Pardon?"

Harper shrugged casually. "Forgive me, but I don't really see the problem. You've found your mate." She held up a finger, stopping Chloe's interruption. "Whether you want to admit it or not." Chloe closed her mouth and let the other woman continue. "And you have a career you enjoy that fulfills you. Why can't you have it all? It doesn't have to be a choice."

Chloe dropped her head in her hands and rubbed her temples for a moment before she answered. "Weren't you listening? I'm investigating claims of environmental mistreatment up here at the Ridge."

"I got that part."

"And I just found evidence of that on the Ridge."

Harper waved her hand in the air. "That's just…whatever."

"But that's the thing," Chloe insisted. "It's *not* just whatever. It's everything."

"It's nothing."

"How can you say that?"

"Because it's not real, Chloe. You must see that."

Chloe shook her head sadly. "What I see is the garbage that was dumped and it came from Grizzly Ridge. That's evidence. Evidence against the Jacksons. Against Luke. It could mean a serious fine. It could mean jail time. It could mean…the end of the Ridge."

Harper laughed. "That's ridiculous."

"No." Chloe stared at her until the laughter dried up. "It's not, Harper. I have to report what I found and depending on how serious it's determined to be, there are all kinds of consequences that could come from this. I don't want there to be, but there are."

She didn't answer right away. Instead, Harper took her time enjoying her coffee, blowing on it and sipping it carefully before she finally looked at Chloe again. "I guess that's true," she said simply. "Unless, of course, you do your job."

Chloe recoiled as if she'd been slapped. "That's exactly what I'm doing."

"I don't think so."

"It is, Harper. My job is to investigate claims of environmental mistreatment."

"And up until yesterday you found how many examples of that?"

"Well, none."

"Right. And then you happened to stumble upon a few bags of garbage by Luke's favorite fishing hole. Seems like a strange coincidence, don't you think?"

Chloe shook her head. "I don't understand."

"Then maybe that's the problem." Harper pushed her chair back and moved to stand. "If you don't understand what I'm saying, then maybe it's time you stopped thinking with your heart and started thinking with your head."

Her head spun. She wasn't thinking with her heart. That was the problem. She wanted to. She wanted to protect Luke, to keep him and his family from whatever trouble there was going to be because of what she'd discovered. She wanted to protect herself. And the love she'd just begun to convince herself could be real.

"The way I see it," Harper continued, "you're so worried about what this discovery is going to cost you—that's why you're thinking with your heart. But if you opened your eyes for a minute, and put your feelings away, you'd see that you've missed some very important details. Details that are way too coincidental, if you ask me." She stood then and looked down at Chloe. "Put your feelings aside and figure out what's really going on and you might just be able to have everything you want after all."

#

When he finally calmed down long enough to talk to Brian Blackwood, it hadn't taken longer than about ten minutes for Luke to get the story of the garbage and the environmental investigation out. It had taken a lot less than that to realize Brian had absolutely no idea what he was talking about.

"You really didn't know about it?"

Brian shook his head, and Luke could see in his eyes he was telling the truth. Also, it was at least the third time he'd asked the question. If Blackwood was lying, he would have sensed it, muddled instincts or not. Besides, wolves weren't known for their dishonesty as a general rule, and the Jacksons had never had an issue with them before. Luke sat back in his chair.

"I believe you," he said after a moment. "But if you didn't know anything about it, or weren't the source of the complaint that brought Chloe out here, then who was?"

"And who dropped the garbage?"

Luke sat up in his chair again. "Exactly. Because there's no way in hell we did it."

"Of course there's not." Brian lounged in his chair with his hands behind his head. "It doesn't make any sense at all for you guys to dump trash on your own land. The land that's your livelihood."

"The land we love."

"Right."

"None of this adds up." Luke couldn't sit any longer. He'd been so sure that Brian would know something; the fact that he didn't was both a relief and a letdown because he was no further ahead than when he'd left the ridge that morning. And definitely no closer to an answer to give Chloe. "I just don't understand it," he muttered as he paced the small office. "Chloe found our letterhead in the bags, which beyond the fact that we would never dump on our land, doesn't make sense because we shred everything we have that uses our letterhead. It's a privacy thing."

Brian nodded.

"So who—"

"Hey boss, I wanted to talk to you about—Oh, I didn't know you had company." A man who looked like a younger, scrawnier version of Brian popped into the office, but the moment he saw Luke, his face hardened and his eyes narrowed. "Is there a problem?" He pointedly looked away from Luke and focused on Brian.

Brian took his time unfolding himself from his chair, but when he stood, Luke could much more clearly see both the similarities between the men as well as the differences. "Luke, this is Darryl Ackerman. My cousin from down south. Darryl, meet Luke Jackson, one of the brothers who runs Grizzly Ridge. The Jacksons are our neighbors."

For at least the hundredth time, Luke wished his instincts weren't still so muddled by his damn mate. Or lack of mating, whatever the case may be, because there was something off about this man. He just couldn't pin it down. He offered Darryl his hand, but the younger man tucked both of his in his back pockets and nodded.

"I know who you are."

Instead of reprimanding his cousin, Brian simply raised his eyebrows slightly before his face returned to neutral, but Luke hadn't missed either Darryl's rudeness or Brian's reaction.

"Well, it's the first I've heard of you." Luke crossed his arms over his chest. "What brings you to Blackwood Ranch?"

"Darryl was getting into a little trouble down in Wyoming, so I brought him up here to work for me for a bit. Thought a bit of hard work could sort him out."

"Is that right?"

Brian nodded.

"And how's that working out for you?"

"Let's just say, Darryl's going to learn a lot in his time here."

The younger man shifted anxiously from foot to foot, and Luke's instincts were on high alert. There was something shifty about this kid, and more than just the fact that he was a wolf. As a general rule, Luke didn't have much time for wolves, but this one really rubbed him the wrong way.

"Right." Darryl sidestepped his way to the door. "I'm sure I will. I should go."

The second he was gone, Luke turned to Brian. "Your cousin has a lot to learn about manners."

"He has a lot to learn, period. But he's a good kid."

Luke didn't think so. "I'll take your word for it, Blackwood. But only because you and me, we're good."

"We are good, Jackson. I don't know what's going on over there on the ridge, but you have my word, it's not me or my guys."

"Are you sure about that? How many men do you have working for you? How many *cousins*?"

"Tread carefully, Jackson. I don't like what you're implying."

Luke held up his hands and stepped backward. "I'm not implying a thing. I'm just saying, something's going on up on our ridge. Something that is beginning to look a lot like sabotage and there aren't a lot of options to choose from here. That's all I'm saying."

Brian nodded and extended his hand, which Luke took.

"I get it, Luke. I'd be the same way if it was happening on the ranch. I'll keep my eyes open around here. You have my word."

It was the best he could hope for.

CHAPTER NINE

"Think with your head, Chloe." She repeated the words to herself. "Think with your head." She'd lost count as to how many times she'd repeated the phrase. Since leaving the Den and her little chat with Harper, it had become her new mantra.

Think with your head.

It's exactly what she'd thought she'd been doing, but it was easy to see now that she'd been working so hard to keep her feelings for Luke from clouding her judgment, she was doing the exact opposite. She so badly wanted what she found to not be connected with Luke and the Jacksons that she wasn't allowing herself to look at it logically and impartially. It was kind of backward thinking, but she was still doing what she said she'd never do again: letting her emotions guide her work.

She'd sifted through the bags again. And separated everything she found into two piles.

There was the kitchen garbage. The organics.

And then there was the paper. Grizzly Ridge letterhead, with nothing written or typed. Just plain paper that had been crumpled into balls. That in itself was strange. Who threw away perfectly good letterhead? The other thing that was strange was…that was it for paper: no receipts, no evidence of shredding, no printed emails. Nothing.

When she looked at it logically, she had to admit, it looked strange. Very strange.

"Think with your head, Chloe."

She moved away from the pile of paper and back to the organics pile. Everything in this bag looked as if it had come directly from the kitchen. And all of it was compostable. Luke had mentioned something about Kade starting a compost pile. She'd go check with him just as soon as she was done. But there had to be something else. Something she was missing.

She needed a break.

What she really needed was to let her bear out and go for a run in the forest to clear her head. But it wasn't a good idea. After all, that's what got her into this mess in the first place. Well, not really, but if she hadn't been in her bear form playing in the woods that day when she'd come across Luke, would they still have the attraction to each other? Deep down she knew the answer was yes. She knew he was right. Harper was right. Dammit, everyone was right. *They were fated mates.* It wouldn't have mattered whether they'd seen each other for the first time in a bar over drinks, or covered in manure in the back of a barn. The attraction would still be just as strong. There was no getting away from it.

With a sigh, she twisted the top off her water bottle and drank deeply. She needed to stop thinking about Luke. She needed to focus. Because the sooner she could solve this little mystery and file her report, the sooner she could get away from the Ridge and him. And that's exactly what she needed to do. If this little incident had taught her anything, it had definitely taught her that she'd been right. A mate was nothing but trouble. She couldn't think clearly, she couldn't work, she couldn't function. If that's what it meant to have a man in her life, she didn't want it.

Determined to get back on track, Chloe pulled out her notebook and read through the notes she'd made. Everything up until that point had pointed only to Grizzly Ridge being on the cutting edge of environmental concern. There had been no red flags. If anything, everything had pointed *away* from them. Which was why her garbage discovery didn't make any sense. Her instinct said it was a setup, but she couldn't file that in her report. Not without evidence. She needed evidence that it wasn't the Jacksons; otherwise, she just couldn't ignore it. She'd have to report it, even if it didn't make sense.

And that would mean a consequence. Probably a fine, a big one, but maybe even jail time, depending on the prosecutor.

Footsteps approaching outside the shed alerted Chloe that she wasn't alone. Her body reacted instantly to the idea that it might be Luke coming to find her again. But she knew better. He'd said his good-bye. And that's what it was: a good-bye. It had felt so final in so many ways, her heart ached just thinking about their last time together. When Kade came around the corner, she was both relieved and disappointed that it wasn't his older brother.

"Find anything?"

She shook her head. "Not yet." She tossed her notebook on the table behind her and made room for Kade on the bench where she sat. He reached past her and grabbed the notebook, which had fallen open to the inside of the front cover. To the picture of little Jordan Adams.

"Who's this?" Kade picked up the notebook before she could grab it back. "He yours?"

"No," she answered quickly. "He wasn't…I didn't…" Chloe swallowed and let out a long sigh. "I didn't even know him. He was a kid on a case I worked a few years ago."

"You deal with a lot of kids in your line of work?"

Chloe shook her head. "Almost none." She took the notebook back from him and stared at the picture. It had been a long time since she talked about Jordan Adams. In fact, she couldn't remember ever actually talking about him. Mostly she'd just tucked away the memories. It was easier that way. She glanced at Kade out of the corner of her eye. He sat patiently, waiting for her to say more. Maybe it was time she did start talking? It couldn't hurt.

"He was different." Chloe ran her finger along the side of the picture the way she had a hundred, maybe a thousand times before. "He lived in the town where I was working on an investigation. My first one, actually." She paused, but Kade didn't push. After a moment, she continued. "I was with a team. We were hired by the town to test the water supply in their new spray park. I was pretty new so I got all the grunt jobs like actually collecting the samples. I knew right away there was something not right. The water…it didn't look right and it had a smell to it on hot days."

"And so you found something?"

Chloe shook her head slowly. "No. We didn't. Or at least my team didn't find anything."

"But if you said the—"

"I know. I couldn't figure it out. I ran the tests over and over. Even after hours, I'd go back and do it again. I was so certain there was something wrong with the water, but I was new and very green and…"

"Nobody would listen to you?"

"Exactly." She nodded. "I couldn't help but think that maybe if I looked a little harder, if I'd done my job better, I would have found something that would have been conclusive. But I didn't."

"And?"

"And we were wrong. The water was contaminated with bacteria. Ten kids got sick. Nine were lucky. Jordan Adams wasn't."

Luke should have headed straight up to the Den to find Axel and Kade and get to the bottom of what was going on. His meeting with Blackwood had done one thing, and that was concrete the idea in his head that even if Brian didn't know exactly what was going on, something was definitely going on and it involved the Blackwood Ranch. The sooner they got to the bottom of what was going on, the better. Especially because as long as the Ridge was under suspicion, it made things way too complicated between him and Chloe, and that was one situation he was not willing to accept.

Despite his resolve to talk with his brothers, Luke found himself taking a left off the path that led to the Den, and instead, led directly to where he knew he would find Chloe. There were a million reasons he should stay away from her and keep his distance, not the least of which was the little coupling they'd shared the day before. That was supposed to be their good-bye. It had been their good-bye in so many ways. But not in the way that really counted. Because there was no good-bye that would ever be good enough, strong enough to make him stay away. He knew that now. Hell, he'd known that then. She was like a magnet that he couldn't pull away from. It didn't matter what she'd found in the woods, or what it could mean to Grizzly Ridge. None of that mattered, and not just because he knew they were innocent of any and all wrongdoing. No, it didn't matter because now that he'd found her, there was no way he was going to let her walk away from him and out of her life. He was going to walk right into that shed, wrap her in his arms and—

Voices.

Luke stopped behind the shed and listened. At first it sounded as if Chloe was talking to herself, but then...*Kade.*

"You deal with a lot of kids in your line of work?" Kade asked.

"Almost none." Chloe's voice was filled with sadness, and something else. *Relief.* As if she had something she needed to say.

Luke forced himself to stay put and listen, unwilling to interrupt her as she started to tell her story.

His heart cracked a little for her as he heard the details of her story: not because it was sad, but because it clearly had made a significant impact on Chloe. An impact that had shaped her career, and obviously her life.

Her voice cracked as the story progressed. Luke could sense her hurting. He could feel her pain, even though he couldn't see her. When she said, "Ten kids got sick. Nine were lucky. Jordan Adams wasn't," he couldn't wait any longer. He moved around the outside of the wall, but neither Chloe nor Kade saw him.

"But you did your job. You tested the samples," Kade said.

"No. That's the thing. The samples were switched. The senior researcher on the team had been paid off. But I should have known. I was the one who collected them. I should have realized they weren't the same. It was my fault."

"Bullshit."

Chloe and Kade both turned to see him there.

"Luke? What—"

"That's bullshit, Chloe." He strode across the space and pulled her from the table and into his arms, taking the notebook out of her hands as he did so. "You did your job. If the samples were switched, it wasn't because of anything you did. You did everything you could."

She shook her head against his shoulder, but didn't speak. Soon, the cotton of his t-shirt grew damp where she rested her head. He didn't press her; he just rubbed her back and kept repeating himself. "You did everything you could."

"They got sick." Her voice was thick and muffled, but he could hear her loud and clear. Kade sat silently, watching and listening with a respect Luke didn't know his little brother was capable of. "All those kids." She lifted her head a little to look at his face. "They were just playing the way kids should and they got sick because someone got greedy."

"It wasn't your fault."

She shook her head. "I could have stopped it. I should have looked harder. I should have seen something. I should have done my job."

"You *did* do your job."

She shook her head again. "He died, Luke."

"I know, babe." He rubbed her back gently and let her fold into him while she cried and finally let out the emotion she'd obviously been holding onto for far too long. "I know. But it's nothing you did. It wasn't your fault."

"And more importantly," Kade chimed in, "this case isn't like that one. No one is going to die because you found a few bags by the stream."

Chloe looked up and used the back of her hand to wipe her eyes before she stared at Kade. A few moments went by before she blinked, and Luke was getting a little worried that she might either start crying again or worse, was going to go after Kade. There was no telling what an emotional bear would do. Never mind an emotional *female* bear. He tightened his grip on her. Not so much to protect her, but to protect his little brother from what could be an emotional, unreasonable female.

But he needn't have worried because the noise that came out of Chloe wasn't a growl or a sob, but...*a laugh?*

"Chloe? What?" He held her out at arm's length to look at her, and sure enough, her beautiful face, streaked with the tears still, was crumpled up in laughter. "Chloe?" He said her name again. "Are you...are you okay?"

The woman was clearly losing her mind. The stress and emotion was getting to her.

"He's right," she said after a moment. "Kade's right. No one is going to die because I found a few bags by the stream." She burst out into a fresh round of giggles and Kade joined in. All Luke could do was stand back to watch and wait it out. She needed the emotional release; he let her have it because he knew enough about women to know what would follow.

Sure enough, it didn't take long before Chloe looked at him and he could see the shift in her moments before the tears started to flow once more. He held out his arms and wrapped her up once more.

"You're right," he said into her ear. "No one will die, but we still need to figure out what's going on. And you're just the woman to do that." He kissed her cheek, knowing it was breaking every spoken and unspoken rule they'd ever had between them, but he no longer cared.

"Luke."

She was so close, he could take her lips into a kiss and she wouldn't have time to pull away, to deny him what he wanted so badly. What he needed. Hell, what they *both* needed. And he was ready to do just that, when her eyes lifted to something just past his shoulder. Her whole body tensed in his arms and he, too, turned to see what she was looking at.

"How could I miss that?" She moved toward the table, and he made no motion to stop her. "It was right there."

"What?"

"I don't see anything." Kade jumped up from where he sat on the picnic table. Luke had almost forgotten he was there. "What are you looking at?"

"That paper." Chloe crouched on the ground by the large table where the contents of the garbage bags were spread out. "Hold on." She reached farther under the table and pulled out a folded piece of yellow lined paper.

Once she stood again, Kade and Luke both gathered around her and watched her unfold it. "It looks like a list of names," she said.

"No." Luke shook his head. "Not just names. Horses." He clapped his hands together. "Blackwood's horses. We got 'em. This was in the bags?"

She nodded.

"You've found it, Chloe. It's the missing puzzle piece and just the proof we need that we've been set up."

"Wait." Chloe shook her head. "I'm not sure about all this. I mean, a setup? I don't understand. Why would someone go to all that trouble? And how would they know I'd find the garbage?"

"They must have known you were here," Kade said.

"Why *are* you here?" The moment he said the words, he wanted to take them back. "I mean...you know what I mean, Chloe. But who hired you? Why did they want you to investigate the Ridge? We never really got to the bottom of that."

"It's not uncommon when a new business starts up," she said. "Especially one that's in such a remote and natural area. It's fairly standard, really. Especially when we get a call."

"A call?" Both brothers asked her at the same time.

Chloe nodded slowly. "From what my supervisor told me, they got a call from someone about the Ridge. I don't know much more than that. But it wasn't the Blackwoods or I would have said something when you mentioned them."

"Who was it?" The hair on the back of Luke's neck stood up while Chloe flipped through her journal to locate the name.

"I was right," she said. "It wasn't a Blackwood. It was a D. Ackerman."

"*D*?" Luke's hands clenched into fists. "As in Darryl?"

"I suppose." Chloe shrugged. "Do you know a Darryl?"

Luke nodded. "Darryl Ackerman." The name tasted bitter on his tongue. "Cousin to Brian Blackwood," he said to Kade. "I met him this morning at the ranch. Apparently he's a bit of a troublemaker and Brian's trying to straighten him out."

Kade crossed his arms and nodded in Luke's direction.

"I think maybe it's time we helped out in that department, don't you?"

"Forget it, Luke. It's a bad idea."

He squeezed his hands together to keep from lashing out at Axel. After discovering the note, Luke had all the evidence he needed to confront Brian again and put an end to things before they got out of control. But Kade insisted they talk to Axel first to let him in on what they'd found. It didn't seem like a bad idea at the time—especially considering it had come from Kade, who was usually the hothead of the three—but now that he stood in front of his older brother, who didn't seem nearly as ready to deal with the problem as he was, Luke started to think he should have followed his instincts from the start and dealt with things himself.

"It's your instincts," his brother said.

"What?" *Had he been speaking out loud? How could Axel know what he was thinking?*

"Your instincts," Axel said again. "They're clouded."

Kade nodded in agreement.

"What do you know about it?" he roared at his younger brother. This was insane. They were wasting time. He could have taken care of things by now if his brothers hadn't insisted on *talking* about everything so damn much. He paced in front of the fireplace. Just being inside was aggravating him. His bear was ready to be unleashed and dammit, those wolves were going to pay for trying to set him up.

"I know you're a mess." Kade laughed. It was a good thing Axel stood beside him, with reflexes quicker than Luke could react, or Kade would have been flat on his back with a very angry bear on top of him.

"Say that again." Luke bared his teeth and struggled against his brother's grip. "I dare you."

"Put your bear away, big brother." Kade patted him on the chest before he had the good sense to take a step back to put a bit more distance between them. "I'm on your side, remember?"

"We're all on the same damn side." Axel pulled tighter on Luke's arms. "Pull it together," he growled. "This is exactly what I'm talking about. Your bear needs to be reined in. And fast."

Luke forced himself to take a breath and try to relax a little bit. Kade might be an ass, but he had a point. He *was* a mess. But as soon as he sorted out the Blackwood situation, he'd be fine.

"You need to take Chloe as your mate."

"What?" He was so shocked, the rest of the tension drained out of Luke, and Axel released him. "What are you talking about?"

"Your instincts are clouded. You can barely control your bear. You're not thinking clearly. You're a complete disaster." Axel held up a hand when Luke took exception to the last part. "You are," he said again. "You're worse than I was before I mated with Harper. It's that in-between stage. You have her, your bears are connected, but until you seal the deal, you won't be operating properly. It's like a fog."

He shook his head, but there was no point protesting it too hard. He knew Axel was right. And it was only getting worse the more time that went by. The need he had for her went far beyond the physical. "I can't." He shook his head again. "We had a deal. It was supposed to stay casual. She doesn't want anything else. Neither did I."

"*Did* you?"

"You know me," Luke tried to explain. "I didn't want a mate. It was never even on my radar. Not really." He shrugged. The truth was, although he wasn't as open to the idea of mating as Axel, he also wasn't as adamantly opposed to it as Kade had been. Luke had always been somewhere on the fence when it came to the idea of a mate, which was why it hadn't been a hard promise to make to Chloe. Not at first.

"And now?" Kade asked.

"Now...I want her so badly it physically hurts inside." It was the truth. The more time that went by with her there—being near her, being inside her, having her in his arms—it just made everything more intense. He wanted her and not just for a night or two, but forever.

Axel nodded knowingly but it was Kade who said, "Do it."

Both Axel and Luke turned to their little brother in shock. Kade had always been adamantly against mating and especially the idea of fated mates because as far as he was concerned, they ruined lives. Or at least, it had ruined their lives when their grandfather had cast out their mother because she'd chosen a mate—their father—from a clan he deemed unacceptable. It was the exact same reason Kade's twin sister, Kira, had been cast out of the Jackson clan. And of course the consequence of her brothers not bringing her back had been for them to be cast out as well. Which was the entire reason the Jackson brothers found themselves on the ridge, trying to make a new life. Everything bad that had ever happened to them had been because of fated mates.

But as Luke was coming to see, there could also be a lot of good.

"I'm sorry, what did you say?" Luke stared at Kade. *Could he be changing his attitude?* "Did you really tell me to take a mate?"

"Not any mate," Kade grumbled. "Chloe."

"And that's different, how?"

"Because you need to. Axel's right—it's screwing with you. Fix it."

Luke needed a moment to process. He turned and walked toward the big picture window that overlooked the clearing where Harper and Chloe were currently gathered around the fire pit with the guests. Harper was passing out roasting sticks and Chloe followed with a bag of marshmallows. She was laughing and from a distance, anyone would believe she was relaxed and carefree, but Luke could see the tension in her shoulders, and the way she looked as if she held the stress of the world. His heart ached to see her so weighed down with worry because of everything that had been happening. Her job was important to her, but he knew he was important to her, too. Even if she didn't want to admit it to anyone. Especially herself.

"I can't." He spoke the words as he watched the woman he loved hold her own roasting stick over the flames. "I can't do it."

"What?" Axel came up beside him. "Why not?"

"Exactly." Kade joined him on the other side, and together they watched the scene outside. "She's obviously in love with you."

Kade's words couldn't have been more unexpected if he'd just told Luke *he* was getting married. He stared at his brother, but Kade wouldn't make eye contact. "What did you say?"

"Anyone can see it." Kade shrugged casually, as if he hadn't just shocked his brothers into silence. "Even me. She loves you, man. I saw the way she looked at you when she was telling her story. And the way you held her. That's love on both sides. Flat out. So I don't see the problem."

"As crazy as it is to say this," Axel ran his hands through his hair and shook his head in bewilderment, "I agree with Kade. Harper and I were talking about it, too. She's in love with you. And we already know you're so stupidly in love with her that you can barely remember your name. So seal the deal, brother."

Luke focused on Chloe again and watched while she bit into the marshmallow and then laughed as the sticky mess trailed from her mouth to her fingers. "She made it very clear that she didn't want anything to do with a mate," he said. "I have to respect that. Her career is too important to her. It's her life. I can't mess with that just because of something I'm feeling."

"She's feeling it too."

"But I promised her. I—"

"That's bullshit and the stupidest fucking thing I've ever heard." Kade grabbed him by the shoulder and turned him so Luke faced him. "And that's saying something considering I spend my days with the two of you. But I've had enough. You love her and she loves you. Mate already. More so we can get on with this whole bloody Blackwood problem and shut it down before it becomes serious. Because if you think for a second that we can handle this with you all screwed up and your instincts all muddled, you're wrong. So, if for no other reason, mate Chloe so we can save her career and the goddamn ridge!" Kade shook his head and slapped his palm against the window so hard it rattled the pane and drew some glances from the women. "This whole discussion is pissing me off. I've gotta get out of here."

Luke and Axel watched as their little brother stormed out the front door, slamming it behind him to take off to places unknown. He wouldn't shift; they knew that much. Kade never shifted anymore. Not since Kira left. Whatever he was going to do, hopefully it put him in a better mood when he got back.

"So," Axel said after a moment. "Looks like you have some work to do. We'll figure out everything else in the morning."

He wanted nothing more than to make Chloe his mate, but Luke also knew he had to do it the right way. "I guess there's only one problem." His gaze traveled back to her. "Chloe."

"I guess you're just going to have to seduce her." Axel slapped him on the shoulder and chuckled. "You've got your work cut out for you, little brother."

CHAPTER TEN

When Luke had asked her to dinner, Chloe's first response was to turn it down. After all, things were complicated enough and she had way more feelings toward him than she should. Especially considering the situation they were in now. And even though it was clear that Grizzly Ridge had been set up with the trash, it was still complicated. And it didn't negate the fact that Chloe still didn't want to get involved with anyone.

Yes, she definitely should have turned down his invite. But she didn't.

"It doesn't mean anything, Chloe. It's just dinner with a friend. In his cabin." She glanced around the path to see whether anyone had heard her talking to herself, but no one was around. The last of the guests had left after the campfire earlier in the afternoon, and Harper said they weren't expecting anyone for two days. Still, she kept her thoughts to herself as she finished the short walk to Luke's private cabin. She hadn't been there yet, but she knew very well which was his. The closer she got, the more she could feel her body hum with expectation.

She could deny it all she wanted, and she did want to. Mostly. But there was definitely some sort of instinctual attraction between them. It was impossible to deny.

It still doesn't mean anything.

She'd put a little extra care into her appearance, brushing out her hair from its usual braid and changing from her field jeans and t-shirt to simple black leggings and a long blue blouse that she knew complemented her eyes. She straightened her blouse now and checked for stray hairs escaping the clip she'd twisted her hair up into on the back of her head.

There was no point in drawing it out any longer. With a deep breath, Chloe reached out and knocked on the door, but it opened, leaving her arm hanging in front of her.

"I'm glad you made it."

She couldn't answer right away because her voice had been completely stolen by the appearance of Luke in front of her. She was so used to seeing him a little on the scruffier side, in worn-out jeans and a flannel shirt or basic t-shirt, that she was totally unprepared for the clean-shaven, neatly dressed, ridiculously handsome man only inches from her. His hair, still damp from the shower, was combed back and Chloe had to clench her hands together to keep from reaching out and mussing it up. Not because she didn't like the way he looked, but because she found it increasingly harder not to touch him.

Even with the crisp scent of the soap on his skin, when Chloe inhaled all she could smell was Luke's unique scent that made her bear go crazy with need. She swallowed hard and took a step back.

Luke's hand shot out and grabbed her arm. "Don't go."

"I...I wasn't..."

She didn't know what she was going to do. But the feelings and sensations flooding her were getting way too intense to keep standing in one spot.

"Come in."

She nodded dumbly and stepped forward, letting him lead her into his cabin. Her skin burned from his touch, even through her blouse, but the last thing she wanted was for him to let go.

Chloe used the opportunity to look around and distract herself from the situation. His cabin was a lot more put together than she would have expected from him. It was simple, but decorated in an outdoorsy way that she would have expected. A big brown leather couch with a matching chair sat in front of a stone fireplace; a pine table was tucked in one corner and shelves lined one wall. The back corner opened into a small kitchen and on the wall next to it was the door she assumed led to the bedroom. It was closed, and Chloe was more than fine with that. She drifted naturally toward the shelves; there were a few books in a stack, mostly about fishing or guidebooks for hikes in the area. But it was the framed photographs that caught her attention. Chloe moved away from him, her arm instantly feeling the absence of his touch, as she picked up the first frame.

"My family."

Chloe nodded and let her finger trail over the glass. The picture was faded and old; the kids were little. Luke couldn't have been more than two or three. Axel, slightly older, stood behind him holding a baby about six or seven months old with a bow on her head, but behind both boys were what Chloe assumed were their parents. Their mother was gorgeous. Tall and slim, with long brown hair that fell over one shoulder. She held the other baby in her arms, Kade. But it was their father who drew her attention. It was easy to see where Axel's looks came from. The tallest and darkest of all the brothers, he was a carbon copy of his dad.

"This is a beautiful picture." She turned to look at Luke, whose face gave away nothing. He never talked about his family, but from the little she had learned, their parents had given them up to the patriarch of the Jackson clan, their mother's father. There was no real reason for it, except a vague explanation of their grandfather not approving of their mother's mate.

Luke shrugged. "It was taken right before we went to live with the clan. It's the only picture of all of us. I like to look at it sometimes."

"Of course. That makes sense."

"I think it's important to remember that while it can be destructive and ruin lives, there's also a lot of good that can come from love and fated mates."

Her mouth dropped open. "What?"

Luke shrugged again and reached for her. "Surprised?"

She nodded and let him pull her close.

"I never said I was against mating. That's Kade."

"But you—"

"I only said I didn't think I'd ever need a mate. Or find one. And I guess, I didn't really know what it was all about. I mean, I'd seen it happen to Kira. And then more recently, to Axel and Harper, but it's different, when…you know."

She did know, but instead of answering him, she swallowed hard and turned her attention back to the photo. "Well, it's a nice photo. And you're right: a lot of good came from their love." Chloe turned in his arms, forcing him to release her as she put the picture back on the shelf. "Something smells really good." It was safer to change the subject completely. "What did Kade make?"

"Kade?" Luke scoffed, pretending to be offended. "My little brother isn't the only chef around here, you know." She followed him into the tiny kitchen and leaned against the counter while Luke finished prepping the dinner that was smelling better and better. "In fact, I'm the only one of us who has a kitchen in their cabin."

"Really?"

"Don't sound so surprised." He took out a ladle and spooned some sauce over the fish in the pan. "I love to cook, but to be fair, I don't do it very often these days."

"Why is that?"

"I only like to cook fish or meat I caught myself, and there hasn't been as much time lately to go hunting or fishing." He dipped his finger into the sauce before he stuck it in his mouth. He added a bit more salt and tasted again, this time smiling. "Perfect."

It was perfect.

She glanced away before she could let the thought stick.

"I hope you're hungry." With expertise, Luke plated the fish over rice and laid some carrots alongside. It looked delicious and Chloe's mouth watered a little.

"Starving." She sat at the table and he presented the plate with a flourish that made her laugh. "So you caught this yourself?" She pointed at the fish and waited while he poured them each a glass of wine before he sat across from her.

"I did. I went up this afternoon." He grinned. "After you agreed to dinner."

"That didn't take long. You got lucky."

"Not yet." He winked and she couldn't help but laugh. "Kidding. And yes, some of it's luck, but it's also knowing your stream. At any rate, I got them pretty quick and had lots of time to get ready for you. Are you going to taste it or what?"

"Right." She slid her knife through the soft flesh of the fish and scooped up a bite on her fork. Chloe had been hoping it would taste as good as it smelled, and she wasn't disappointed. It was better. "Luke, this is...oh my goodness. What is that?"

He took a bite before he answered. "It's just a garlic

lemon butter sauce. Damn, that is good." He smiled, obviously pleased with himself, and took another bite. "It's best to keep it simple and really let the flavors of the fish shine through."

"Well, it really is delicious. Thank you."

Luke put his fork down. "No." His tone turned serious. "Thank *you*. I didn't think you'd agree to come here tonight. I'm glad you did."

Chloe reached across the table and took his hand before she answered as honestly as possible. "I'm glad too."

He couldn't have asked for a better night. Well, maybe he could. But the night wasn't over yet.

After finishing their dinner, Chloe agreed to share another glass of wine, and they'd moved to the couch, where she curled up her legs and got comfortable. Luke would have liked to help her get a whole lot more comfortable, but he was a patient man. Sometimes.

Their conversation had moved easily and by the time they were done with their second glass of wine, they'd talked about their childhoods, places they'd traveled, and places they'd like to go. He was more confident than ever that Chloe was the only one for him and he'd meant what he'd said to her earlier. He'd never been against the idea of mating. Not really. Sure, he'd given Axel a hard time when he'd first found Harper, but that was different. Mostly, he just had no idea how it would feel when it happened to him.

And it most definitely had happened to him.

There was no way he was going to let this woman walk out of his cabin and out of his life after her work was done on the Ridge.

No way.

"Luke?"

He blinked and focused on Chloe, who looked at him with a question on her face. It was clear he'd totally missed whatever she'd asked him.

"I was saying that it was a good thing you didn't have guests for a few days since Harper seems so tired lately."

"Does she?"

"You hadn't noticed?" She laughed a little and a strand of hair escaped the clip she had it caught up in. He'd been restraining himself from reaching up and taking the clip out completely to let her hair free. What he wouldn't give to weave his fingers through that silky softness and pull her toward him to kiss her so thoroughly she made that sexy little groan of hers. "Maybe she's been working too hard." Chloe was still talking. "I'd like to do something nice for her. After all, this is…" She waved her hand and changed direction before she could elaborate. "I mean, I haven't been the nicest to her and she's been so good to me. Almost like a friend and Lord knows it would be nice to have—"

"I don't want to talk about Harper."

Chloe closed her mouth slowly. "Oh."

Luke scooted across the couch so their knees almost touched. "Not that I don't love Harper. But what I should have said is, I want to talk about you." He reached out and let his fingers trail along her knee ever so slowly. "You and me."

"Luke, there's no—"

He silenced her with a finger to her mouth. "I don't want to hear it."

She shook her head. "Whether you want to or not, it still needs to be said. I told you when this started what I could and couldn't do, Luke." She started to shift away from him, but he could sense the hesitation in her. He'd been sensing it all night. She was battling with herself. "I told you, no—"

"I'm telling you that it's okay to change your mind."

Chloe started to shake her head and Luke hit his breaking point. He'd been restraining himself all night, but he couldn't keep his hands off her any longer. He moved quickly so he was over her on the couch, trapping her within his arms. "If you can tell me that you don't really feel it, that you don't know with every fiber of your body that to walk out of here and never look back would break you, then I'll go. I'll get up and let you walk out. But I don't think you can do it."

She opened her mouth to speak, but he cut her off.

"Don't lie, Chloe. Don't lie to me. But especially don't lie to yourself. You want this and you can have it. You *can* be happy."

She shook her head so he slid one hand to her cheek and held it.

"You can, Chloe." He kissed her then and almost at once felt her melt against him. "And I'm going to convince you," he murmured against her mouth and kissed her again. Hard.

She groaned, that sexy sound that made his bear come alive, and that was all he needed to hear. Luke scooped her up in his arms and stood.

"Luke, put me down. You—"

"One night, Chloe. Put away all your rules and everything you *think* you want and *should* have and just let yourself feel. If at the end of the night you still feel the same, I'll walk away." He wasn't sure he could, but he knew if she didn't want him as a mate, he'd have to. "But if you're honest with yourself and you think *maybe* this could happen, then…"

Her body trembled in his arms. "Then what?"

"Then you're mine."

Her eyes flared with desire. She bit down on her lower lip for a moment, and finally nodded. "One night."

He growled in response and his dick hardened in his pants. He'd promised one night, but the way she looked at him, he was confident it wouldn't take that long. He strode across the room to the bedroom and kicked open the door. Her eyes widened, and he could have sworn he heard her growl, too.

He tossed her on the bed and she immediately unbuttoned her blouse.

No, it wouldn't take all night, but they had it, so he planned to make full use of it.

Luke crawled up on the bed and on top of her. He stilled her hands and with a quick yank, tore the rest of the buttons of her blouse away to expose the creamy perfect skin of her belly and a blue satin bra that just barely contained her breasts. The full globes straining against the fabric called to him and he wanted nothing more than to bury his face between the perfection of her tits, but there would be time for that later.

With a tug, he pulled her leggings down to her ankles and shed himself of his own clothing.

"There's no way you can know what you do to me." His voice was hoarse and strained as he looked down at his woman—so ready, so perfect, so much his.

She licked her lips before she reached up and with one hand behind his neck, pulled him down to her. "Oh, I think I have a pretty good idea."

Being with Luke was all-consuming. Chloe didn't have time to think about all her reasons for not being with him, because all she could think about was being with him and making it last as long as possible.

Why can't it last forever?

That was the one thought in her head as they came together in their first shattering climax. They worked so well together, especially in the bedroom. Maybe if she'd experienced this type of passion with someone else she wouldn't be so overwhelmed by it.

But maybe the reason she'd never had it before was because…

Because she'd never had Luke.

Chloe curled up against him, letting him pull her close while he kissed the back of her neck and stroked her hair over her shoulder. At some point, it had escaped the clip and lay tangled across her back.

"I like your hair down." Luke twined his fingers through her strands and Chloe was pretty sure she'd never felt anything so sinfully erotic and exquisitely sweet at the same time. "It's so sexy." He left a trail of kisses down her neck. "You're so sexy. Perfect."

It might have been her postcoital bliss, but Chloe couldn't remember the last time she felt so happy and content. As if she was right where she belonged. She snuggled into him a little more, letting her backside rub up seductively. It elicited just the response from him she hoped for.

She knew she was playing with fire. And it wasn't fair to him to lead him on that she'd give him more than one night. He wanted to mate. That much wasn't a secret. He'd made it pretty clear that he wanted her for more than just one night. *He wanted her forever.* Shivers raced through her body at the thought.

In response, Luke pulled her closer and kissed her neck. Her heart clenched in her chest in a way that was painfully perfect.

It felt so right. He felt right.

But forever was a long time.

Forever meant giving up everything she'd worked for with her career. But all that might be gone anyway after all the drama with the setup and the Blackwoods, or whatever it was that was going on, was finished. And even if it wasn't over...

It didn't have to end.

Chloe squeezed her eyes shut as Luke's hand traveled down her bare arm. She was well aware that it was her, not him, who'd put labels and barriers on what was going on between them. And it was totally in her power to put an end to all of them. His hand moved lower, to the dip in her waist, where it rested for a moment. Heat flared through her body at his touch, the way it always did.

It was up to her. What had he said? *Put away all your rules and everything you* think *you want and* should *have and just let yourself feel.*

The problem was...when she did that...when she let herself feel...she knew exactly what she wanted.

"Luke?"

"Um hmm?" His hand moved over her hip and squeezed; his fingers danced on her skin, sending shockwaves to her core.

"About what you said earlier...about one night? About letting myself feel?"

"I remember."

She swallowed hard, hardly able to believe she was about to say what she was going to say.

"I'm feeling."

Her voice was barely more than a whisper, but his hand

stilled on her body.

When he didn't respond right away, Chloe bit her lip and tried to turn her head to see him. "Luke?"

"What is it you feel?" His fingers tightened on her hip, as if she'd bolt. And maybe she would have.

Chloe swallowed hard. "I think you know."

"I want to hear you say it." She felt him move behind her; a moment later, he rolled her onto her back so she looked up into his intense eyes. "Tell me how you feel," he demanded. "Tell me you love me."

"It's...I..." She stumbled over the words because they weren't enough. "I can't," she said.

Luke growled, but she wasn't scared. Her bear was only just under the surface, ready to respond to him in every way.

Chloe propped herself up on her elbows. "But only because it's more than love. You know that. Love is so..."

"Say it, Chloe."

"Love isn't enough to explain how I feel," she blurted and then before she could stop herself, "You're mine, Luke, and I want to be yours."

"Are you saying—"

"I want to mate." Her whole body reacted to the words. "I want to—"

It didn't matter what she was going to say, because he'd already heard all he needed to. He bent and took her mouth with his in a long, hard kiss. *She was his.* And now he was going to make it official. *Permanent.*

Beneath him, Chloe groaned and arched her back up into him.

Luke's bear was only just contained, right beneath the

surface. He couldn't wait.

He needed her.

Now.

But as much as his body ached to take her, he was determined to enjoy every minute of claiming her as his own.

With a hand on each of her hips, he deftly flipped her so she was on her stomach, her perfect, round ass exposed to him.

"Damn, you're gorgeous."

Starting at her neck, he kissed and rubbed his way down her body. Judging by the moans that got increasingly louder, Chloe was enjoying his attentions almost as much as he was. He moved to the soft globes of her ass and kneaded and massaged, occasionally slipping one hand between her legs to tease her clit.

"Luke, I can't take it." She wiggled her hips as she ground herself into the mattress beneath her, seeking release for the pressure he'd built in her.

Without pause, Luke delivered a smack to one cheek, just hard enough to make a point and leave a sweet pink spot that made his dick swell painfully. "I don't think so, babe. Your release will be mine to give."

She twisted her head around; she looked so goddamn sexy with her hair tousled, the need in her eyes heavy and her breath coming in pants, Luke knew he wasn't going to be able to wait much longer. But first, he needed to make her his.

He slipped his hand between her legs again, finding her wetter than before. Knowing how turned on she was only increased his own need for her. She squeezed her eyes shut and groaned at his touch. He slid one finger inside her wet heat, and then another, rotating slowly. Torturously slowly. With his free hand, he rubbed her pink ass and gave it another light smack for good measure. Chloe's body reacted instantly. She was close to climax, but he needed her to wait. Just a little bit longer.

Increasing his rhythm inside her, he bent to kiss the spot he'd reddened on her ass. The moment his lips touched her skin, Chloe's body tensed around his fingers; his bear roared to life and he knew it was time. As she reached her climax and screamed out her release, Luke bit down into her sweet, soft flesh and finally claimed what was his.

CHAPTER ELEVEN

Waking up cuddled into Luke's chest, his arm draped protectively over her, may have been the best thing Chloe had ever experienced. Well, close to the best thing. Her body vibrated just remembering the way they'd come together the night before. The sex between them had always been phenomenal, but last night was different. They were mated, and she wasn't sure how it was possible, but everything between them now—every touch, every kiss, every…everything—was magnified. And finally her thoughts were clear. The cloud that had hung over her, muddling her thoughts ever since she'd met Luke, was gone. Her instincts were crisp once again.

She stretched her arms over her head and tried to wiggle away from Luke so she could slip out without waking him. She moved an inch and his arm squeezed her tight to him.

"Where do you think you're going?"

Chloe rolled over so she was half lying on his chest. "I was going to go see if you had any coffee in that kitchen." She bent to kiss his cheek, but Luke grabbed her face and pulled her in for a completely different kind of good morning kiss.

"Good morning." She drew out the words playfully.

"It absolutely is." Luke squeezed her close again. "There's nothing better than waking up next to you. My mate." His hand slipped down her bare back and cupped her ass gently. "How does it feel?"

She narrowed her eyes in faux anger and smiled. When he'd bitten her the night before, she'd been shocked and also completely overwhelmed with the orgasm it elicited. Sure, she knew what mating entailed, but she hadn't really thought about what it really meant, and she certainly hadn't thought he would choose her ass cheek as his mark.

"It's a little sore."

He rubbed his hand over the spot, gingerly tracing one finger along the tooth marks. "Sorry about that."

"No you're not."

"You're right. I'm not." He grinned and she smacked him lightly against the chest. "You're mine, babe. All mine."

The words once would have caused her panic, but so much had changed in such a short period, and the actual act of mating had left her feeling more content than she'd ever felt in her whole life. "And you're mine."

He growled and with an ease that took her breath from her lungs, flipped her over until he straddled her, his strong arms caging her in. "And the very first thing I'm going to do with my mate is—"

A sharp knock on the front door was followed by Kade's voice. "Luke? Chloe?"

"Shit," Luke grumbled in protest, but didn't move.

"You two better be up." Kade's voice got louder as his footsteps approached. "And you better be decent." There was a sharp rap on the bedroom door and it swung open. "Oh shit." Kade shook his head but didn't look away.

Chloe felt a blush burn up her cheeks, but she knew Luke's body sheltered all but her face from Kade's view.

"I'm going to guess by the...well..." Kade waved his arm in their direction. "Well, are you mated or what?"

"We are. Now if you wouldn't mind, I have things I need to be doing to my mate, if you could close the door on your way out."

Kade bent and picked up a t-shirt from the floor before he threw it at Luke. "No can do, big brother. We have that little matter of the wolves to deal with. I assume you both have clear heads, so we can get started."

Chloe and Luke groaned at the same time.

"I'm sure you guys will survive."

"Give me ten minutes while you get Axel."

"No deal, Luke. Axel isn't coming. Something about Harper being sick."

Chloe was instantly worried about her friend, but Kade kept talking.

"She'll be fine, but Axel thought it was best if he stayed with her. So it's just us."

Chloe patted Luke's chest. "He's right. We'll have time later for...well, for everything."

He kissed her hard and thoroughly. "You bet your sweet ass we will." Right in front of his brother, Luke jumped out of the bed, being sure to keep Chloe covered from Kade's eyes, and pulled the t-shirt over his head before bending for his jeans. "Okay," he said to Kade. "Let's do this. What's the plan?"

"I don't like it."

Luke paced the great room in front of the fireplace. Kade had just laid out the plan for setting up and busting Darryl Ackerman about his role in the setup and Luke didn't like it. Not one bit.

"It's the only way." Axel had joined them for the planning session and Chloe had gone to sit with Harper for a few minutes to let the brothers sort things out.

"Bullshit."

"Okay," Axel conceded. "It's the *best* way."

"No." Luke shook his head. "There's no way I'm letting you put my mate at risk like that. If it were Harper, there's no way you'd let her risk herself like that. And you know it." There had to be a better plan because so far the only thing they'd come up with involved way too much risk on Chloe's part.

"Luke." Kade stepped in front of him, stopping his pacing. "It's the *only* way. It doesn't have to get dangerous."

"It doesn't have—"

"It *won't* get dangerous," Axel jumped in. "I mean really. If this Darryl wanted to take it to that level, he would have. It seems to me that he's taking a very mellow approach to sabotage."

"Mellow?"

Luke felt anything but mellow. Especially if it meant his mate was going to have to be anywhere near the asshole who'd started all of this. He didn't want anything to do with it. Axel was right: now that he'd mated, his instincts were crystal-clear and they roared for him to keep Chloe far away from the wolves.

"Luke, we need to put an end to this right now."

"The sooner the better."

His brothers stood before him, a unified front. Luke trusted them both with his life. He knew they'd never make a decision that would hurt him or his mate. Not intentionally. But that was fine in theory. It was a different thing completely to put into practice now that it wasn't only himself he had to think of. "No." He crossed his arms over his chest in a showdown. "I don't care what the fuck you say. It's not happening. Chloe's not doing it."

"I'm not doing what?" She came up behind him and wrapped her arms around his waist. "What am I not doing?"

"It doesn't—"

"Meeting with Darryl," Kade cut him off. If Chloe hadn't been holding onto him, Luke would have torn his baby brother's head off for saying anything. Kade continued as if he hadn't noticed Luke was ready to take him down. "We have a plan to get Darryl to confess to planting the garbage. It's the easiest way to get it done quickly without much drama."

"But?" Chloe aimed the question to Luke.

It was Axel who answered. "But Luke doesn't think you can handle it."

Luke growled, baring his teeth before he pulled it together. "That's not true," he said to Chloe. "I *know* you can handle it. I just don't want that mangy wolf anywhere near you."

Chloe smiled and swallowed a laugh. "I can do this, Luke." She turned to the brothers. "And if it's the easiest way…"

"It is."

"Then let's do it."

"Chloe, no—"

She spun around so she stood in front of him, and gently tipped his head down to hers. "Luke, I'm a big girl. I can do this." He opened his mouth to object, but as he was doing it, he knew there was no way he would change her mind. She was stubborn and strong and so damn capable. But she was also…*his*. He kissed her hard.

"Okay."

Chloe gave him the sexiest smile and turned around in his arms. "So, what do we have to do?"

He wrapped his arms around her and pressed her to him, but he wouldn't stop her from participating. Not if it was what she really wanted to do.

"It's simple, really," Kade started to lay out the plan. "We're ninety-five percent sure that Darryl Ackerman is behind all this."

"One hundred percent," Luke clarified.

Kade ignored him. "So we'll get you to call him and set up a meeting. Once you meet with him, you'll show him the pictures of the garbage, make up a story about how a team is going to be coming up and doing a further investigation into the Ridge as well as surrounding properties."

"Surrounding properties?"

Axel nodded and stepped forward. "Plant the idea that there was something suspicious in the findings that may link the surrounding properties to the problem. We want to get him flustered so maybe he'll slip up."

"He didn't strike me as exactly the sharpest guy around," Luke said. "He'll panic."

Chloe nodded. "Okay, that sounds simple enough. I assume I'll be recording it all."

"Absolutely. And we'll be right outside to make sure nothing will go wrong."

Luke glared at his little brother. "Nothing *will* go wrong."

"Sounds simple enough." Chloe stepped away from Luke's arms. "Let's get started right away. What are we waiting for?"

It did sound simple. But it was one thing to talk about something and another thing entirely when it was your woman who was the bait. It didn't matter what anyone said—Luke didn't like it.

#

The call was made. Darryl had agreed to meet with Chloe at the Station, the only bar in town. If he'd had his choice, Luke would have chosen any other number of places other than the sleazy bar. But it had been Darryl's choice—of course it had—and when they thought about it, it meant there'd be enough other people around that Darryl wouldn't be able to try anything, and Luke and his brothers would be close enough to step in if anything went sideways.

Not that it would.

But just in case.

Everything was set up and ready to go. Luke had come down to the bar early, to make sure everything was set up and ready to go. Chloe would have to drive herself just in case Darryl happened to see her, and Kade and Axel should be joining him any time. He glanced at his watch again. They still weren't there and the meeting was set to start in less than fifteen minutes.

"Dammit, Kade."

He'd set up camp in the bar's kitchen, and made more than one mental note to never eat there again. He may have enjoyed a plate of nachos once or twice with his brothers, but after seeing firsthand the level of hygiene standards, or in this case, the lack of standards, that wouldn't be happening again. He pulled his cell phone from his pocket and was ready to dial his brother's number when the kitchen door opened and he walked in.

Alone.

"Where's Axel?"

Kade shook his head. "He wouldn't leave Harper. She's throwing up and can't keep anything down. He's almost as bad as you with his mate."

Luke growled, but ignored him. He had enough to worry about. "Did you see Chloe before you left?"

"Oh, I saw her."

"What the hell does that—"

"Look for yourself." Kade deftly dodged his brother and pointed to the swinging door that led to the bar. With a grunt, Luke went to the grimy circle of glass and peered through it for a second before he pushed the door open just enough to get a better look.

"What the hell?" Kade yanked him back into the kitchen. "You can't risk anyone seeing you. Get in here." His little brother shoved him back and Luke had to stuff his hands into his back pockets to keep from hitting him. Or more likely, storming out to the vinyl booth where his woman sat, wearing the tightest, lowest cut shirt he'd ever seen on her. Hell, he could see every curve, even from a distance. It wasn't that he objected to seeing any of her luscious body: he objected to *Darryl* seeing it.

"What is she…where did she…"

"Settle down, big brother, and control your bear before you cause a scene." Kade gestured to the pimple-faced dishwasher who watched them with open curiosity. "She borrowed it from Harper. Something about her best blouse being ruined."

Luke's dick throbbed from the memory of ruining that very blouse. He shook his head and tried to focus. Darryl should be arriving in a moment and the sooner they got this over with, the sooner he could take his mate and get the hell out of here.

He took a breath and paced the kitchen again.

"If you can put your bear away long enough, we can get this done." Kade pulled out his phone. "Let's do a quick test." They'd set Chloe up with a little mic that was linked to an app on both her phone and both of theirs that would allow them to listen in to the conversation but would also record it on her phone so they'd get the evidence they needed.

They opened the apps and immediately the sounds of the bar filled the kitchen. It was loud. Too loud. The brothers looked at each other, both thinking the same thing.

"Hey." Luke waved at a waitress who was loading plates of greasy-looking burgers on her tray. "I need you to do something."

She put the plate she was holding down and stuck her hip out. "I'll do anything you want me to, handsome. Name it."

A wave of something that felt strangely close to nausea washed through him at the idea of any woman who wasn't Chloe doing anything at all to him. "Not like that, sweetheart. I need you to take an order for me."

"I like orders." She lowered her lids and thrust out her tits.

He heard Kade's chuckle behind him. *The little shit was enjoying this.* "No," he said more forcefully. "There's a woman sitting alone in the booth out there and—"

"If you're into that kind of—"

"No." Luke crashed his hands down on the stainless-steel counter but the sound didn't drown out Kade's laughter behind him. He'd deal with him later. "Go take her order for a drink or food or something."

Finally getting the point, the waitress straightened up, her seductive look totally replaced by the anger of being rejected. "Whatever."

"Please," he added, forcing himself to stay calm. "I'm sure my brother here would love to buy you a drink later as a thank-you."

His words had the double and satisfactory result of shutting Kade up and making the waitress happy enough to do his bidding. She blew a kiss in Kade's direction and with her hips swinging widely, left the dinner order behind and sauntered out into the bar.

"I'm going to kill you."

"Whatever." Luke ignored him and turned his attention to his phone again. "Let's see if we can actually hear anything."

Kade swallowed back whatever he was going to say and pulled his own cell phone out.

The eighties metal music muffled most of the voices, but if they listened hard they could sort of make out the waitress asking Chloe whether she wanted anything to drink. Then Chloe's voice, clearer, ordered a Sprite. And then, "Oh. You must be Darryl."

"Hi...you...Chloe...beer...sugar." The brothers looked at each other. The feed was too hard to make out. Kade went to the door and looked through the window. He turned around and nodded at Luke to confirm it. Darryl Ackerman was there and they couldn't hear a damn thing.

The moment he sat down, Chloe knew they had the right guy. Darryl Ackerman was definitely responsible for setting up Grizzly Ridge and the Jackson brothers. She couldn't say how she knew, but her instincts screamed at her that he was not only responsible, but he was also not a good guy. The way he squeezed her hand a little too long when she held it out to him in introduction and then stared a little too long down the cleavage of her shirt didn't help her impression.

"I'm glad you could meet with me, Mr. Ackerman."

"Darryl."

"Darryl," she repeated for the benefit of the recording that she hoped was working. "Darryl Ackerman."

"That's me."

"Right." She took a deep breath and tried to look a lot more relaxed than she felt. She hadn't been nervous at all until the moment he walked into the dodgy bar. She could smell the wolf in him. He was mangy and more than a bit on the wild side. He made the hairs on the back of her neck bristle. But she wouldn't let him see her discomfort. She could do her job. Play her role. "I wanted to talk to you about what I found on the Ridge."

"You found something." It wasn't a question.

"I did," she continued seamlessly and shifted in her seat in an effort to draw his gaze back up to her eyes. She knew Harper's top probably wasn't the best choice for the meeting. But it gave her a good spot to tuck the mic where it wouldn't be muffled and as long as he didn't look too hard, he shouldn't be able to see it nestled between her breasts. It was more than a little disconcerting to have him so openly admiring her body, but Chloe wasn't totally without skills of her own. If he was distracted enough, she could use it to her benefit. She leaned over slightly. Just enough. "But first I wanted to ask you a few questions that might help us understand what exactly we're looking at."

Darryl grunted. The waitress reappeared to deliver Chloe's Sprite and a mug of beer. His gaze momentarily redirected to the waitress's short skirt and barely covered ass. When she'd left, he turned his attention back to Chloe. "What ya wanna know?"

She smiled sweetly and put her notebook on the table in front of her, being careful to squeeze her chest together a little bit as she did so. "The first thing I'd like to know is what your concerns were that prompted you to call us in the first place. Was there something specific that concerned you?"

"Yeah."

Chloe waited a beat, but the answer didn't seem to be forthcoming. "What was that?"

Darryl took a slurp of his beer. "Don't like 'em."

"What's that?"

He put the beer down on the table and leaned forward. "I don't like 'em," he said again. "They're bears."

Chloe almost choked on her drink. It was shifter code. He shouldn't have said anything. It wasn't mentioned. She coughed and cleared her throat hard.

"Settle down, sister. I know you're one, too." He took another loud slurp of beer. A trail of fear slid down her spine. And she sat up straighter. "Didn't know that when I hired you, though."

You can do this, Chloe. She swallowed hard. *Just do your job.* That's all she had to do. Her job. The same way she always did. She had failed Jordan Adams, but she was not going to fail Luke. She wasn't going to fail any of them. She could do it.

"I can assure you, Mr. Ackerman, I wasn't aware of the Jacksons', well…situation when I took the job." That wasn't entirely true. Everyone in the western states knew who the Jackson clan was, but this mangy wolf didn't have to know that. "And it in no way affected my investigation." She pressed her arms closer to her side, pushing her breasts up even further. The move had the exact effect she was looking for. Darryl swallowed hard and Chloe could almost see his mouth start to water. *Apparently wolves like a woman with curves, too.*

She had to forcibly keep herself from shaking in disgust at the thought.

"Yeah, I know."

"You know?"

"You found the trash, didn't you?"

Trash? She hadn't mentioned what she'd found on the

property. Chloe almost squealed in joy. He'd slipped up. Luke was right; he wasn't very sharp, but she hadn't thought it would be that easy. She took a long drink of her Sprite to keep from smiling.

"I did have a finding," she said easily when she put the glass down. "In fact, I think my findings will be very interesting to the state environmental commission. I wouldn't be surprised if they wanted to do a full sweep of the area."

Darryl sat back in the booth and stretched his arm out. "What's that mean?"

"Just that once something is found on a property, often the state likes to conduct a thorough investigation of all the properties in the area to see if there are any other infractions." She was lying through her teeth, but she was fairly confident Darryl wasn't sharp enough to notice. "So I guess that means…" She pretended to look at her notes. "The Blackwood Ranch will need to be notified as well. But I'm sure—"

"The ranch?"

"Of course."

"No." He sat up, crossed his arms over the table and grabbed Chloe's arm, knocking her glass over.

Chloe's first instinct was to pull away and to her surprise, Darryl released her. "Excuse me? Mr. Ackerman. I don't think—"

"I need to show you something."

"Pardon?"

"Something that will change your mind about what you found."

Chloe's mind spun. He was changing tracks so quickly, she could barely keep up. "What I found? You mean the—"

"Trash. Yes."

"I never told you it was trash." She realized a second too late she'd given up her game, but if he noticed, he didn't show it.

"I have more evidence in my truck. But you have to come now. Quietly." He looked pointedly at her chest and raised his bushy eyebrows. "Quietly," he repeated.

There was no way she should go with him. He was a wolf and clearly involved with the sabotage. He could be dangerous. Hadn't Luke warned her about him? He was worried about this whole setup. She fought the urge to glance toward the kitchen, where she knew he'd be watching and waiting with Kade. But he hadn't come out yet, so he must be okay with everything. If it wasn't safe, he would have put a stop to it already.

It must be okay.

"We can't hear anything." Luke paced across the kitchen again. It was making him crazy. They'd been able to hear Chloe a little bit, but then things got muffled again and getting every second word wasn't enough for him to know anything. "This isn't working." He turned to Kade, who nodded and tucked his phone into his back pocket.

"I agree. But I think we got him. At least, we have something and hopefully she's getting something we can use, but—"

"What do you mean, *hopefully*? She'll get what we need to take him down, Kade. My mate is more than capable."

"Simmer the fuck down, Luke. I know Chloe's capable, but I think we should hedge our bets, too. I'm sure the recording is working fine, but just in case, I'm going to get Blackwood so he can hear it from Ackerman's mouth directly. You're sure he has no idea?"

Luke nodded. "He may be a wolf, but Blackwood is straight up. I trust him. He didn't know about this."

"Good. I'll be right back. Don't make a move until we get back. We need Brian to hear it from Ackerman. Got it?"

Luke hesitated.

"Luke? Don't be a hero. You'll only make it worse."

"I'll do what I have to do."

"Bullshit." Kade stared at him. "Stay put. I won't be long."

"No problem." He told his little brother what he wanted to hear but he wasn't making any promises he might not be able to keep.

"Good. You got this?"

Luke nodded again and Kade left. Of course he had this. He wasn't going to let anything happen to his mate and yes, she might be more than capable, but she was still his. And he'd die before he let anything happen to her. He'd resisted the urge to look through the window in case he was spotted. He'd give it another few minutes and then he'd stick his head out. He had to give Chloe the space to do what she needed to do, but five minutes was enough. It was all his bear would allow.

"Where's your truck?"

Darryl walked a few steps in front of her, leading her around the back of the building, and her instincts were going crazy. She never should have let him lead her away from the main street. She was being stupid, and she knew it.

But at the same time, she also knew she could hold her own. Besides, she had backup. She glanced down into her cleavage where she'd hidden the mic. Luke and Kade would be listening. They'd know if she needed help. Which was why despite Darryl telling her she needed to be quiet, she'd started to talk again.

"Why would you park back here? There were lots of—"

"I told you to be quiet." He whirled around and grabbed her arm again. This time he squeezed and yanked her close so he was only inches away and she could smell his stale, beer-soaked breath. With his free hand, he reached into her shirt, between her breasts. Her breath caught in her throat.

"Get your hands off—"

"Just looking for this, sweetheart." He pulled the mic from her bra and let his meaty fingers graze against her breast as he did so. He dropped it to the ground and squished the bug under his heel. "We don't want those bears listening in any more than they should, now do we?"

"They know I'm out here." Chloe tried hard to control her growing panic; a guy like Darryl would only feed off it.

"Maybe." He shrugged. "But what are they going to do? Those stupid bears are more interested in protecting their beloved Ridge than they are about anything else. Especially some scientist lady."

She shook her head. "That's not true."

"Isn't it?" He sneered; his lips pulled back gruesomely over his teeth. "They thought you could get me to come clean about the garbage, isn't that right?"

"Come clean about what?" Her arm ached from his tight grip, but as long as she could keep him talking, she could still get him to admit to everything. And something in his expression gave her an idea. "The trash they hid on their property? Pretty good idea, wasn't it?" Chloe watched as Darryl's face changed from smug to confused. She kept going. "I mean, you gotta think they saved a ton of money by hiding the trash on their property and really, it's so big, no one would really notice. At least they—"

"They didn't do it." Darryl's face twisted in anger. "Bears ain't smart enough to think of that."

Chloe shrugged and did her best to look innocent. "Then who could have thought of such a brilliant plan?" She had to fight the urge to roll her eyes; it was almost too easy.

Predictably, Darryl puffed up his chest and nodded sharply. "I did."

"You put the bags there?"

"I did. Pretty smart, huh?"

She couldn't answer right away because she never would have thought he'd actually admit to it. She prayed that even if the mic was gone, the app Luke had put on her phone was still recording. "Wow," was all she could manage to say.

"That's right. I—wait a minute. Are you trying to set me up?" His face morphed again. His nostrils flared, and she could see the wolf lurking just underneath. She was definitely dealing with an unpredictable shifter. And obviously one without much of a moral code—or any code at all.

Chloe shook her head. "You got rid of the mic, remember?" Her instincts screamed at her to get the hell out of there. "Which means, they're probably on their way out here right now."

"I don't see 'em."

She tried to spin around and look, but Darryl still had her arm in a clench. He spun her back around to face him, this time pulling her tight to his body. Chloe's bear roared with objection inside her. She didn't want to have to shift here. Not like this. *Where was Luke?*

"And ain't that convenient?"

Before Chloe could squirm out of the way, he pressed his wet, sloppy lips to hers and shoved his tongue in her mouth. She pulled back, gagging. Her bear roared and she no longer cared whether she was too exposed: her animal was not going to be contained. But she needed him to let her go. She couldn't shift while he was holding her. She needed space.

"Get your hands off me," she growled.

"Or what?" he taunted her. "You been spending too much time up on the Ridge. Time you knew what a real man was—"

She shoved his chest, hard. Hard enough that he released her arm and stumbled backward into the garbage bins. It wasn't much, but it might give her enough time to shift.

"Bitch!" he yelled behind her, but she didn't look. Not until she heard a growl. A growl that sounded way too much like a wolf.

Her muscles twitched, and she turned, ready to shift.

But there wasn't time. As she flew backward against the wall, she thought Darryl stunk like a wet dog who'd been rolling in the garbage; as her head hit the brick wall, Chloe's last thoughts went to Luke.

Luke burst out into the bar, his eyes going directly to the booth Chloe had been sitting in. *Empty.*

He'd been waiting, listening in vain and waiting. But when he'd heard her voice in his mind, calling for him, there was no way in hell he was going to stand by and do nothing. His instincts were out of control. His mate needed him and now, as he stood in the musty bar, staring at the empty booth, he cursed himself. He never should have waited so long.

The parking lot was empty. The sun, starting to set behind the mountains, cast strange shadows along the few cars that were parked there.

No Chloe.

She was in trouble. He knew it with every fiber in his body, just the way he knew that if that mangy wolf had anything to do with it, he'd rip it apart. Luke focused and sniffed the air. She was close.

He followed the scent of his mate around the side of the building and immediately his vision clouded over with rage at what he found. Ackerman, or the wolf he assumed to be Ackerman, stood over his mate. She was knocked unconscious, but Luke knew she was breathing. As for Ackerman, his breath was going to be limited.

Very limited.

Without bothering to remove his clothes, Luke shifted at the same moment he lunged toward the wolf. The dog turned and looked at him, his lips pulling back over yellow canines in a snarl before he, too, charged.

The two animals met in a flurry of fur, teeth, and claws.

A sharp pain burned Luke's back leg, but he barely registered the wound as he dove again for Ackerman. Normally an alpha bear and wolf might be an even match, but there was no way Darryl was remotely close to alpha of his pack, never mind the fury of an alpha bear whose mate had been threatened. It didn't take long for Luke to gain the upper hand in the fight.

With a swipe of his paw, he sent the dog flying into the wall, where he landed with a hard crack, but Luke was out for blood. And he wasn't going to be satisfied until he had it. He stalked over to his prey and pulled him out into the open.

"Luke!"

Somewhere through his rage, he heard his brother's voice behind him but he was focused. He stood on his hind legs and let out a roar that shook the ground around him. No one hurt his mate and Luke was going to make damn sure he made that clear. He bared his teeth and eyed the dirty fur that covered the wolf's neck.

"Stop!"

Luke froze. *Chloe.*

He turned his heavy head and looked into Chloe's eyes. Brian and Kade helped her stand and she leaned on Kade for support. "Don't, Luke. Don't hurt him."

He growled.

"He's not worth it."

Luke looked back to Darryl, who'd shifted back into his human form. He looked even more pathetic lying naked on the ground, fear blazing in his eyes, blood dripping from his shoulder and face. Luke growled again and turned, his eyes locked on his mate.

"He admitted everything," she said.

"You can't prove anything, bitch."

Without looking, Luke swiped a paw in Darryl's direction and tossed him like a rag doll a few feet away, where he landed with a thud.

"You deserved that, asshole," Kade said.

Luke stalked over to his prey, still not convinced he should spare the idiot.

"I recorded it on my phone," Chloe said. "It's all here." She held up her phone.

"Is it true?" Blackwood walked over to where his cousin lay and looked down at him. "Did you do it? Did you betray our friends?"

"Friends?" Darryl spat and sat up. "They're bears. And they're taking your business. I did what I had to."

"You're an idiot," Brian said. "I should let you end him

right now." He looked at Luke, who was still ready to finish the job.

He wanted to. He wanted nothing more than to raise his paw and wipe the lowlife right out of existence. He looked over at his mate. She waited. He knew she wouldn't try to stop him. She knew him too well. Even though they hadn't even known each other a month, she knew him. More than anyone ever had, Chloe knew him. The very heart of him. And although she knew him well enough to know that if he needed to take care of Ackerman in order to feel as though he'd handled the situation, that's what he needed to do. But judging by the look in her eyes, she also knew that he wouldn't do it.

He couldn't. Not for this. But if he ever laid a hand on his mate again, the situation might be different.

With one more look in Chloe's direction, Luke turned back to his victim lying beneath him. He raised a heavy paw and with tempered force, swung at Darryl, who went skittering across the pavement and into a pile of garbage bags. Satisfied with the noise the wolf made, Luke made his way around the corner and to his truck, where he'd left a spare set of clothes.

CHAPTER TWELVE

December

When Chloe decided to surprise Luke by catching an earlier flight so she would be home two days earlier, she hadn't factored in what the weather in Montana in December could be like. She was thankful that she decided to rent a Jeep at the airport to make the drive. The four-wheel drive was definitely coming in handy as she navigated the treacherous mountain roads on the way to Grizzly Ridge. But despite the danger the snow brought, it sure was gorgeous. And nothing was more Christmasy than a snowy mountain lodge.

It was certainly different from the last holiday season she'd spent holed up in a hotel room in Florida. She could have gone home, but it seemed easier to stay and work instead of dealing with the questions from her family about why she was still single and working all the time. This Christmas would be different. Very different. In only a few weeks, Chloe would be spending her very first Christmas as a mated woman.

It still sounded so strange to her, but it definitely didn't feel strange. In the few months that she and Luke had mated and made the decision for her to stay at the Ridge with him, everything felt right. Really right. Especially now as she pulled the Jeep into the snow-filled driveway in front of the Den.

The lights were already on even though it was still early, but with the snow landing on the peaks of the log building, covering the lights, the glow was magical. She could picture the oversized tree they'd put up the week before she'd left. They'd all gone out in the woods to cut it down together and spent the rest of the day decorating. Chloe had never felt such a sense of family as she had with the Jackson clan. She could picture them now, probably spending the afternoon all enjoying an afternoon of no guests, sitting by the fireplace in the main room.

And that's just where she was headed.

She left her bags in the Jeep and picked her way through the building snow to the main door of the Den. Just as she'd expected, the fire was going when she opened the door.

"Hello?"

Chloe had barely gotten in the front door when Harper jumped up from the couch and ran to her, pulling her into a huge hug.

"You're back! And early, too." She squeezed Chloe tighter than she would have thought possible. "You're so sneaky."

Chloe wiggled her way out of Harper's embrace. "I don't know about sneaky. But I did want to try to surprise Luke. Where is he?" She tried to sneak a glance over the other woman's shoulder.

Harper waved her arm in the air. "He's in the kitchen. They're having a brother meeting. Something about Kade needing help and not wanting it. Axel got sick of him complaining so he put an ad out for a cook."

"No way." For all the complaining Kade did about his time in the kitchen, everyone knew he also took a great deal of pride in his work there, too. Chloe couldn't imagine that he'd be very excited about having someone else come in and take over. "How'd he take that?"

"About as well as you'd expect." Harper laughed and yanked Chloe's hand. "Now come sit and tell me about your trip. We'll only have a few minutes before Luke realizes you're here and drags you off to your cabin to have his way with you, and I'll lose all chance for girl talk."

Chloe laughed because it was both true and an exaggeration. Luke would most definitely drag her off—at least, if she had her way—but she also did plan to have a lot of time for girl talk. At least until after Christmas, when she'd be traveling again. But she let Harper pull her to the couch anyway. They'd become even closer once Chloe moved to the Ridge and once they got over their initial rocky start when Chloe had been less than friendly with her. As it turned out, Harper was more than willing to overlook it, especially considering she also hadn't been herself.

Harper rubbed her stomach and sat on the couch next to Chloe.

"How are you feeling?" It turned out that when everyone else was busy taking down Ackerman, Harper was bedridden with the worst morning sickness anyone had ever seen. Of course, they didn't know that until afterward and she took a pregnancy test. The whole thing had come as a surprise, for no one more than Harper herself. "You look so much better." Chloe slapped a hand to her mouth. "Not that you didn't look amazing before, but—"

"I know what you mean. And I did look terrible."

Harper laughed. "Let me tell you, this little cub is certainly putting the love of a mother to the test long before he makes his appearance."

"It's a—"

"We don't actually know yet. It's too early. But I have a feeling he'll be just like his father." Tears sprang to Harper's eyes and she didn't bother to wipe them away.

"Harper." Chloe jumped up and handed her friend a tissue. "What's wrong? Is everything okay?"

Her friend waved her hand, dismissing her tears, and she blew loudly into the tissue. "I'm fine. It's just…well, I didn't think I'd ever be able to have a cub, you know? I mean, I'm only half-blooded and Axel's just so happy. A doting dad already. It's all so overwhelming. Especially because pregnancy hormones are nothing to be messed with, especially when you're pregnant with a bear."

Chloe laughed. "I can't even imagine."

"But you will, right?" Harper's hand clamped down on Chloe's arm. "I mean, you guys will have cubs, won't you?"

She couldn't answer her friend, because the truth was, she hadn't thought of it. At least not in any real sense. She'd been so busy just spending time with Luke and finding the balance between work life and home life that she hadn't considered adding anything else into the mix. The idea wasn't totally off-putting, however; not the way it would have been six months ago. But a lot had changed, and judging by the warm feeling growing in the pit of her stomach at the idea of having a cub of her own, obviously her opinion on children had changed as well.

"Harper, Axel wants to—"

The women swung their heads around at the sound of Luke's voice. The words died on his lips when he saw Chloe and a smile split across his face. She jumped up and ran to him, happy to be back in his arms.

He held her tight and kissed her hard as if he hadn't set eyes on her in months instead of only a week. "What are you doing here? I thought you weren't coming back for two more days?"

"I wanted to surprise you."

"Well, you did." He kissed her nose and let his hands slide down to her backside and his mark the way they always did. "And I couldn't be happier about it."

He kissed her again and Chloe let her hands slide up into his hair to hold him even closer. She never failed to heat up immediately for him. He sparked something in her that had never before been lit and she was definitely not in a hurry to douse that flame.

"Get a room, you two."

She'd totally forgotten about Harper. Chloe pulled away, but didn't let go of her man. "Happily."

Harper laughed. "Go for it. But first, what were you going to tell me, Luke?"

Luke's eyes clouded with confusion for a moment before they cleared as he remembered his purpose of coming to talk to her. "Right. I was going to tell you that Axel wanted you to help him in the kitchen. Kade got mad and stormed out, so it's just going to be us for dinner, and…" He drifted off, looking into Chloe's eyes. "Correction," he said. "It will only be you two for dinner. I think Chloe and I can cook something up ourselves."

"I'm sure you can." Harper shook her head and pushed up from the couch. "You guys shouldn't have let Kade out there on his own, though. The storm's getting worse."

"I'm afraid that whatever's going on outside doesn't come close to the storm waging inside him." The concern for his little brother weighed heavily on Luke. It did on both of the Jackson brothers. But Kade was the only one who'd be able to help himself. And that was only if he decided he wanted help. Until then, there was nothing anyone could do.

"Well, I'll leave you two alone and go get my mate to cook something up for me and his cub." Harper rubbed her tummy again and gave Chloe's arm a quick squeeze as she passed. "I'm glad you're home."

When Harper was gone, Luke pulled Chloe back into his arms. "I'm glad you're home, too. I missed you." Their kiss was slow and sweet. "I always miss you."

"I always come home," she said. "And I always will."

"It makes me so happy to know the Ridge has become home for you."

"Of course. I love it here and more importantly, I love you and your brothers and Harper. And I'm going to love all the little cubs running around, too."

"Cubs?" He raised an eyebrow at her.

The little warm glow in her tummy lit up again and before she could stop herself, she said, "Well, maybe one day we could..."

Luke laughed. "Cubs?"

She nodded. "Think you could handle it?"

"Little versions of you and me running around?" He shook his head, but the grin on his face gave him away. "I think I could handle it." He squeezed her bottom again, his thumb tracing the lines of his mark through the fabric of her pants. "One day, yes. But right now I definitely have my hands full, don't you think?"

Chloe reached up and kissed him full on the mouth. "I wouldn't have it any other way."

THE END

If you enjoyed His to Seduce you'll love Luke's story, His to Claim, coming Spring 2016!

Make sure you visit Elena Aitken on her website at:
www.elenaaitken.com

And hang out with her on her Facebook page for up-to-date information on the release of this new series.

https://www.facebook.com/elenaaitken.author

I have the best job in the world because I get to write the stories of my heart and it's my hope that you enjoy reading them as much as I love writing them. Whenever I get the chance, I escape to the mountains to soak up the inspiration and plot my next story.

To learn more about Elena Aitken and her other books, please visit www.elenaaitken.com
Twitter - @elenaaitken
Facebook - www.facebook.com/elenaaitken.author

His to Protect

Please enjoy this exclusive *raw* unedited excerpt from His to Claim, the third book in the Bears of Grizzly Ridge Series, coming late spring 2016!

His to Protect

CHAPTER 1

For Chloe Karrington there was nothing better than walking through the forest. The way the sun danced and played in the branches of the pines as she walked, the cushion of the needles beneath her feet, the fresh, crisp air she inhaled deeply into her lungs.

No. There was nothing better than a walk through the forest.

Unless it was a run.

She glanced around. She was alone.

She could shift into her bear. The need to release her animal bristled just below the surface, but she pushed it down. There were certain things she could do, and certain things she couldn't. And letting her bear loose in an unknown forest was most definitely in the *couldn't* category.

But maybe…

She let her mind drift as she checked our her surroundings.

There was no one around. And she already knew there were bears on Grizzly Ridge. Beside the obviousness of the name, it was well known in the bear community that the Jackson brothers had been exiled from their clan and had settled on the ridge instead. Besides, no one would see her if she was careful.

"No." She stamped her foot to make her point. "Pull it together, Chloe. You're working."

She straightened her shoulders, and flipped her dark braid over her shoulder. If there was one thing Chloe prided herself on, it was her professionalism. As an environmental impact researcher, she took her job extremely seriously. Especially since the very thing she always seemed to find herself researching was the very habitat she craved the most. That, and if she did screw up, the ramifications could be very serious. Maybe even life threatening. Chloe flipped open her leather bound notebook and stared at the newspaper clipping she'd taped into the cover as a constant reminder.

Her fingers traced the faded photo of little Jordan Adams.

Only five years old.

Yes, she reminded herself. There were consequences to making mistakes. Mistakes she'd never make again.

She liked to be reminded of the past, but only to the extent that it kept her on her toes. Mostly, Chloe was happy to put the past behind her. *Way* behind her. She tucked the book back into the canvas cross body bag she always wore and continued walking.

It was more than just a recreational hike, but more of a recognizance mission as she made her first journey out onto Grizzly Ridge. Later that afternoon, Chloe would drive up the road, park in front of the buildings and formally introduce herself to the Jackson brothers that ran the adventure tourism lodge on the ridge, but for the moment she was enjoying the peace and allowing herself to form her own opinion of the operation. It was a technique she liked to use whenever she had the opportunity. Besides, there was a chance that as soon as she made it known that she was there to investigate complaints of environmental disruption, she might not be Grizzly Ridge's most popular guest. And the opportunity to investigate the area on her own would definitely be gone.

She walked for a few more minutes, letting her mind clear. It didn't take long for Chloe's bear to sneak up toward the surface of her consciousness again. How long had it been since she'd run?

Weeks? Months?

Too long. *Way* too long.

Ironically, she'd originally taken the job because of the ability to be outdoors. It had seemed like a good way to satisfy the animal inside her. What she hadn't anticipated was that despite the time outdoors, there was less time to let her bear out than she'd thought. But, as it turned out, there were other benefits to the job. Like being alone. Her family would like nothing more than to see her settle down and have her own cubs. Chloe was lucky her parents weren't traditional in their thinking. They were more than happy for her to pick her own mate.

As long as she picked one.

She shook her head.

The last thing she needed was someone tying her down, telling her what to do and keeping her barefoot and pregnant.

No thanks.

Ever since she was little, Chloe had been fiercely independent. She could handle herself, and that's exactly what she did. She saw the way her older cousins and sisters changed themselves for the males in their life. Becoming giggly and stupid, pretending they couldn't open jars of pickles. *What was that all about?* She could open her own jar of pickles thank you very much.

No male needed.

Not that her parents understood that. Which is why her career was perfect. She moved around so much from one job to the next that she'd effectively made herself a very undesirable partner. After all, not many strong, alpha males liked a woman with a serious career. At least none she'd found.

It was the perfect explanation for her mom and dad and for the most part they seemed to understand, even if they couldn't totally wrap their heads around the idea that Chloe was choosing to be alone.

The thing was, as much as she didn't want to admit it, even to herself…Chloe didn't want to be alone. Not really.

She was so wrapped up in her thoughts as she walked, Chloe hardly noticed that the thick pines were thinning. Not until she stepped out onto the ridge. The blue of the sky stretched out before her, the view of the mountain range took her breath away.

"Wow." Was all she could manage to say. It was woefully understated, but there was no word to describe the incredible beauty mother nature had laid out before her.

Stunned into silencing her mind, Chloe stood frozen on the ridge and took it all in.

After a few moments of admiring the view, she made a split second decision. It wasn't the most responsible thing to do, but…screw responsible. She needed to experience this amazing place in all the glory it really had to offer. And there was only one way she knew to do that.

She was careful to fold her clothes and her tuck her bag next to a tree. Then, naked, Chloe took a step and stretched her arms up overhead. The moments before she shifted into her bear had always been the only time Chloe was comfortable in her curvy human body. Her thick thighs, and ample chest were nothing but a hindrance in her daily life, but in those moments, they felt almost sensuous. And then, a second later, Chloe exhaled and started running. As she moved, her body morphed seamlessly into a strong, beautiful black bear.

Chloe pushed every thought from her mind and let her lean muscles stretch with the exertion of the run. The cool wind on the ridge whipped through her fur and the feeling of freedom that flowed through every fibre in her body made her feel alive in a way that nothing else had in months.

Soon, she veered from the ridge and into the cover of the trees where she scratched her back against the trunk of a tall pine before rolling in the fragrant forest floor. She was so caught up in herself, she didn't hear the animal approaching until it was too late.

Luke Jackson stared directly into the bluest eyes he'd ever seen on a black bear. Not that he saw many black bears on his ridge. Or, any at all.

The bear hadn't heard him coming but the moment she had, she'd flipped over from where she was rolling in the pine needles like a cub and stared him down, baring her teeth to him with a snarl. The fact that there was a strange female black bear who was maybe half the size of his own massive grizzly, and that female was standing her ground against him, intrigued Luke. A lot.

But not as much as the scent of her. Fresh and crisp like the pine trees they were surrounded by. But something else, too. A white musk that filled the air, and his senses.

Which is why it took him a moment to react the way he should have immediately. Finally, his senses caught up with him. With a roar, Luke reared up on his hind legs in a move that was more threatening than predatory, but he knew it would serve his purpose and scare the intruder away, which is exactly what it did. By the time he'd dropped to all fours, the black bear was gone and to his shock, Luke was disappointed.

Very disappointed.

Luke's role at Grizzly Ridge, the eco-adventure lodge he and his two brothers had opened a few months before, was to lead the hikes and outdoor activities. A perfect fit for him since he'd always felt more at home in the woods that anywhere else. It also meant that he could legitimately sneak away to shift into his bear and run free as frequently as he needed too. Especially now that it was autumn, also known as *bump season*. There weren't many guests for the next few weeks, and the few they had at the moment seemed to be more interested in staying close to the main lodge, also known as the Den.

With his free time, he was supposed to be working on a new fly fishing tour they were going to start offering to guests, but that afternoon Luke couldn't resist the urge to let his bear run. As soon as he'd shifted and his senses were heightened, he recognized that something was different. There was an unrecognizable scent. Another bear. He knew the woods better than anyone. Every sound, every shadow…every scent.

And the scent of a female was definitely unusual on Grizzly Ridge. A few months earlier his older brother, Axel had taken a mate. Luke had recognized right away that Harper was at least part bear, but she'd been totally unaware of it and had never shifted before until after she and Axel had mated. Once she'd discovered her bear, there was no keeping her away from it. Axel and Harper spent a lot of late nights running through the woods. But the scent Luke was picking up on was definitely different than Harper's slightly sweeter smell.

This female was different. His blood ran hotter with every breath in. She filled his senses.

It hadn't taken long to track her. If she'd been trying to hide, she'd done a bad job of it. Luke approached quietly, stalking her. It was always best to tread lightly until one knew what he was dealing with. But when he saw what he *was* dealing with—a black bear who for all intents and purposes looked like she was *playing*. He wasn't sure how to handle it.

And she wasn't just any black bear. She had the most magnificent, shiny dark fur that he'd ever seen. It almost appeared blue where the sun hit it. But not as blue as her eyes. Never before had Luke seen a bear with blue eyes and when she finally noticed him and her gaze locked on his, those eyes flashed with electricity. But it wasn't fear. It was almost a challenge.

A challenge he'd accepted. Although moments after he reared up and roared, causing her to run, he'd regretted it. It was probably for the best. At least that's what Luke kept telling himself as he turned and lumbered back in the direction he'd come from. Back to the Den.

Nothing good could come from a female bear. Particularly one that clouded his senses so quickly and completely the way that little black bear had.

No. It was definitely better that she'd run off.

I hope you enjoyed that little sneak peek!

51203860R00103

Made in the USA
Lexington, KY
15 April 2016